me you us

me you us

WITHDRAWN

AARON KARO

Simon Pulse

New York   London   Toronto   Sydney   New Delhi

SIMON PULSE

An imprint of Simon & Schuster Children's Publishing Division
1230 Avenue of the Americas, New York, New York 10020
First Simon Pulse paperback edition June 2016
Text copyright © 2015 by Aaron Karo
Cover illustration by Jessica Handelman
Cover illustration copyright © 2016 by Simon & Schuster, Inc.
Also available in a Simon Pulse hardcover edition.
All rights reserved, including the right of reproduction
in whole or in part in any form.
SIMON PULSE and colophon are registered
trademarks of Simon & Schuster, Inc.
For information about special discounts for bulk purchases,
please contact Simon & Schuster Special Sales at 1-866-506-1949
or business@simonandschuster.com.
The Simon & Schuster Speakers Bureau can bring
authors to your live event. For more information or to book an event
contact the Simon & Schuster Speakers Bureau at 1-866-248-3049
or visit our website at www.simonspeakers.com.
Cover designed by Jessica Handelman
Interior designed by Mike Rosamilia
The text of this book was set in Scala.
Manufactured in the United States of America
2 4 6 8 10 9 7 5 3 1
Library of Congress Control Number 2015933770
ISBN 978-1-4814-4063-9 (hc)
ISBN 978-1-4814-4064-6 (pbk)
ISBN 978-1-4814-6877-0 (eBook)
This title was previously published as *Galgorithm*.

For Mom and Dad,
Patron Saints of Patience

1

THE KEY TO A GIRL'S HEART is through her eyelashes.

That's what I tell all the guys who come to me for advice. If you don't know what to say to a girl, if you're talking to a girl and start to panic—hell, if you accidentally hit a girl with your car and are cradling her in your arms until the paramedics arrive—the next words out of your mouth should always be a compliment about her eyelashes.

"I really like your eyelashes."

"Your eyelashes are pretty."

"Wow, your eyelashes are so long."

Honestly, it doesn't matter what you actually say. As long as you look in the general vicinity of her face, speak in an upbeat, positive tone, and manage to get out the word "eyelashes," you're on your way.

Upon hearing this advice, a lot of guys respond, "That's a weird thing to say. I've never even *noticed* a girl's eyelashes before."

To which I reply: *"Exactly."*

According to my calculations, at Kingsview High School a girl is hit on approximately three to seven times per day. There are many ways to get her attention: The jocks are flexing their muscles. The hipsters are sending her music. The preps are liking her Insta.

But not a single guy is complimenting her eyelashes.

The fact that you even *acknowledged* her eyelashes, that you had the guts to utter this praise out loud, *to her*, will immediately make you stand out.

Because, let's face it: You're not a jock. You're not a hipster. You're not a prep. If you've come to me for help, you're a nobody. Just another anonymous and involuntarily celibate teenage guy who could use some guidance.

You may have heard my name, Shane Chambliss, whispered in the desolate, sexless hallways between AP Microeconomics and AP Physics and thought my services were a myth. But I can assure you that if I decide to take your case—and only the most desperate qualify—I will be your savior.

Because while in most respects I'm a totally normal high school senior, one thing sets me apart: I know girls. I know how they think. I know what they want. And though they may seem like baffling creatures who speak another language, I will help you engage with them genuinely and thoughtfully.

Acquiring this expertise took time. I've spent the last few years carefully logging and codifying every interaction I've observed between guys and girls. Myself, my classmates, strangers in the mall—they all became my test subjects; their responses, my data. Every pickup line and rejection has been cataloged and quantified. Every tip and move has been stress-tested and tweaked.

And after all this research and painstaking fine-tuning, I have finally developed a proprietary formula that will help you approach, woo, and win over the girl of your dreams. I call it the Galgorithm.

If I take you on as a client, you will gain access to my knowledge and the laws of attraction outlined in the Galgorithm. It will help you cultivate a deep, personal connection with the girl you've been pining after. It is your map on the road to a fulfilling relationship.

I don't charge. After all, helping the romantically challenged isn't a job to me; it's a calling. In exchange for my services, I only ask one thing: Keep my methods and my role as your mentor a secret at all costs.

Some of the lessons I impart to you may seem silly or obvious. But I can assure you that they have worked on sorrier cases than yours.

The first set of tasks is the simplest but can also be the most daunting:

- Be different.
- Notice her.
- Tell her.

The first one shouldn't be difficult. You *are* different. You're weird as hell. That's why girls don't talk to you in the first place. But don't think of it as a disadvantage. Think of it as an advantage. Leverage your weirdness to stand out.

Next: Notice her. I mean *really* notice her—and I don't mean her body. I'm sure you've more than noticed that already. I'm sure you've noticed it alone in your bedroom late at night. But that's amateur hour. I need you to take her in: her smell, her clothes, her presence. Every girl is unique, but you need to discover what is unique about *her*.

And, finally, tell her. All the moves in the Galgorithm won't help you a lick if you never actually use them. At some point, this girl, this fellow human being you've held up on a pedestal for so long—well, buddy, you're eventually gonna have to go right up to her and say something.

Be different. Notice her. Tell her.

That's where it all begins.

And if nothing else works, you always have your fail-safe, your watchword, your mantra . . .

Eyelashes.

2

ONE DAY REED WANAMAKER could be president of the United States. He could own a yacht. He could host a beauty pageant. He could do all those things if he only saw the potential in himself that I see in him. Unfortunately, that isn't the case. Right now Reed Wanamaker is pathetic.

I'm currently sitting with him in the high school cafeteria. While we enjoy our lunch, an eager squirrel does the same ten feet away—but that's not strange at all. Kingsview is a leafy suburb of Los Angeles, and here the notions of "inside" and "outside" are totally blurred. Yes, Reed and I are inside the school . . . but we're also outside. Some of the hallways have no ceiling. The cafeteria has an awning but no walls.

Reed is extremely skinny—like past the point of scrawniness and into awkward *Is he okay?* territory. I know it's not because he doesn't eat—he's already polishing off his second grilled cheese. Reed simply lost the genetic lottery and was born with the skeletal structure of a paper clip. He also has ears like open car doors and stick-straight light brown hair that seems to have not one but two parts. I still believe in him.

"So where are we with Marisol?" I ask.

"You're not gonna believe this," Reed says. "She accepted my friend request! Huzzah!"

"What did you just say?"

"She accepted my friend request!"

"No, after that."

"Huzzah?"

"Yeah."

"You know, 'huzzah!' Like 'hooray!'"

"Reed, remember how I never steer you wrong?"

"Yeah . . ."

"Here's a tip: Never say 'huzzah' ever again. Or 'hooray,' for that matter."

Reed considers this. "Noted."

When Reed says "noted," he means *noted*. He jots down my admonition in the little notebook he carries with him everywhere. I'm not sure if he's absorbed anything I've taught him so far, but at least he's noted it.

"So what's next?" I ask.

The object of Reed's affections is Marisol Cuéllar, who, as it turns out, is standing across the cafeteria from us, chatting with some friends. Marisol's looks are severe: midnight-black hair pulled back tight into a ponytail, dark eyebrows that zag instead of curve away from the bridge of her angular nose, and a pair of razor-sharp elbows. She and Reed are both juniors. It may be tough, but I think I can make this work.

"What do you mean, what's next?" Reed says, flustered.

"I'm just kidding," I say. "But it's been a little while since we caught up."

We've recently returned to school from "winter" break—winter in quotation marks because it was seventy degrees and sunny almost every day. Incidentally, our return to school also marks the beginning of the home stretch of my senior year. Six months from now I'll be wearing a royal blue cap and gown. I'm deep in the throes of denial, but that's a sentiment for another time.

"Take me back to the beginning," I say.

"Well," he says, "at first, Marisol didn't even know I existed."

"Reed."

"Right, right, sorry."

"Reed!"

"Right . . . right, *not* sorry."

Two more tips I offer new clients: Be positive as much as possible, and apologize as little as possible.

For instance, Reed claims Marisol didn't even know he existed. Even if that were true in a class of only about two hundred and fifty kids, there's no use dwelling on it because she definitely knows who he is *now*.

Reed also needs to shed his habit of saying he's sorry all the time. Only apologize when it's warranted; otherwise it seems like you're apologizing for being yourself.

"Anyway," Reed continues, "me and Marisol had never even spoken until I hit her with a tennis ball during gym."

That was Reed's idea. Phys ed is the only class he and Marisol share, and he felt it would be a more "organic" approach if, during tennis instruction, he hit her with a ball. I knew Reed's puny arms could never generate enough force to leave a mark on Marisol. Hell, I'm impressed he could even hold a racket, let alone swing one. But sure as Cupid's arrow, he hit his target, albeit meekly in the thigh. It was an odd move for sure, but that's why I admired his moxie.

"So you hit her with a tennis ball . . . ," I say.

"Right, and then I went up to her to ask if she was okay." Reed pauses for dramatic effect. "And that's when *I* got pegged in the face by Harrison."

Harrison Fisk, a senior like me, is the starting pitcher for the baseball team and a full-time troublemaker in the off-season. He spotted Reed on the court during phys ed and for unknown reasons took the opportunity to fire a tennis ball at him from close range.

"I got a bloody nose and had to go to the nurse."

"I love this story," I say.

It's true. I *do* love this story. Because Reed, with a little unsolicited help from Harrison, followed to a tee my first guideline: Be different. Over the course of her life, Marisol will receive flowers from more suitors than she'll be able to keep track of. But she'll never forget the beanpole who tagged her with a tennis ball and then got whacked in the face while checking on her. Mission: accomplished.

"What happened next?" I ask.

"You said to send her a friend request within thirty-six hours."

The Galgorithm dictates that the optimal window for establishing social media contact after a first encounter is more than a day, so as not to seem eager, but less than two days, so as to still be top of mind.

"How long did it take her to accept your request?" I ask.

Reed consults his notebook. "Six hours. Just before we went on break."

"Wow," I say. "That's quick."

"Really?" Reed says. He's pumped up and can barely contain his excitement. And that pumps me up as well. To me, there's nothing better than a happy nerd. It's what gets me out of bed in the morning.

"Are you ready for the next step?" I ask.

"Shane, I've been ready for the next step since I hit puberty."

I look him up and down. Puberty couldn't have been that long ago.

We both spy Marisol across the cafeteria. Maybe fifty feet away from us. It's not a huge distance in physical terms. But romantically, she might as well be living on Jupiter.

It's my job to help Reed get to Jupiter.

3

IN MY OPINION, THERE IS a spectrum of best friendship. At one end is "just met and totally hit it off." At the other end is "known each other for so long that we have a baby picture in the bathtub together." The latter describes me and Jak. Our mothers are best friends, so from the time we were born, we've been inseparable. The coed baths have stopped, but we're still just as close.

She came into the world as Jennifer Annabelle Kalkland, but everyone calls her by her initials: *JAK*.

Having been raised in the orbit of car-crazy Los Angeles, we stopped walking and started driving everywhere as soon as we were old enough to get our licenses. That all changed over winter break, though, when Jak got us both Fitbit fitness trackers as Christmas gifts. Currently she's making us walk home from school in an effort to maximize our total steps for the day. I welcome the competition, but only because it gives us more time to dish on the latest gossip in Kingsview.

"Remember that party I was telling you about, with all the baseball players?" Jak asks.

"Yup," I say.

"I heard that Harrison and Rebecca Larabie hooked up. It's real DL."

Harrison is the aforementioned jock who bloodied Reed's nose. Rebecca is also a senior and your classic overachiever: AP everything, school president. The girl has her own business cards.

"No way," I say.

"Yes way," Jak replies.

"I don't believe they hooked up."

"Shane, why would I make something like that up?"

"Because you have a vivid imagination and a lot of time on your hands."

Jak takes umbrage at this. "I do not have a lot of time on my hands!" She wags her finger aggressively in my face. "That's totally bogus!" She continues pointing at me, almost touching my nose.

"Wait a minute," I say. "I know what you're doing!" I grab her arm and attempt to halt the finger wagging. "You're trying to run up your Fitbit score!" We both glance at the lime-green electronic bracelet on her wrist. She wriggles out of my grasp.

"No I'm not!"

"Jak, it doesn't work like that. It won't count as a step if you just wave your wrist around. Otherwise I'd—"

"Otherwise you'd what? Rack up two miles every night around eleven thirty?"

We both grin. Touché.

"Anyway," I say, returning to the point, "Harrison and Rebecca? Seems like a weird combo."

I would never expect a straight shooter like Rebecca to go for a loose cannon like Harrison. Which just goes to show: Even if you've spent years studying them, the inner workings of girls' hearts are still mysterious.

"Agreed," Jak says. "I don't see it."

Jak knows I help a few clueless guys at school talk to girls and score dates, but she has no idea about the extent of my endeavors. I've never told her anything about the Galgorithm. I guess there was just never the right time or place to clue her in . . . and I'm also a little scared she'd judge me for it. Jak does not pull punches.

"How do you think they got together?" I ask, referring to Harrison and Rebecca.

"Alcohol, most likely," Jak says.

"Ah. Alcohol. I should have thought of that."

"Oh yeah," Jak continues, "it's the ultimate social lubricant."

"Gross."

Jak ignores me and instead begins to shuffle her feet,

taking one step back for every two steps forward and slowing our pace down to a crawl. I shake my head.

"Jak, you can't fool the Fitbit. You're never gonna beat me."

"That's what they told Beyoncé and the Wright Brothers."

Jak cracks me up. She soon abandons the shuffle and resumes walking normally, which means she now covers more ground than me. It's those long legs of hers, which are poured into her usual skintight jeans and filthy white low-top Chucks.

"Are you looking at my legs?"

I snap out of it. "What? No."

Jak grins. "I need to tweet: 'Just caught Shane Chambliss looking at my legs. #busted.'"

"I was not looking at your legs!"

Jak laughs. She loves to push my buttons.

"Go easy, Chambliss. I'm just messin' with you."

"I know, I know," I say with a smile.

Jak pulls her hair in front of her face in order to inspect it. She prides herself on not having cut her mess of black hair in years. It's gone from full-on Afro to dreadlocks to a style that could now only be described as curly chaos.

"Who's gonna walk you home in the fall when we're away at school?" she asks suddenly.

Bit of an odd question. Jak usually doesn't like to talk about Life After High School. We both got into college Early Decision last month, otherwise joyous accomplishments marred by the fact that we'll be a thousand miles away from each other. We've tried to avoid the topic ever since.

"First of all, don't you mean who is gonna walk *you* home from school?"

"Let's be clear," Jak says. "I'm walking *you*, not the other way around. America."

I laugh. "Huh?"

"You know." Jak smirks. "We're progressive."

"Whatever you say."

I try to tell myself it's not that big a deal to be apart for the first time from the best friend I've had since our days in Jak's bathtub. Between the half dozen video-messaging apps we have on our phones already, I'll probably see her more often than I do now. I've almost got myself convinced.

We reach the corner where we go our separate ways to get home. Our neighborhood is full of quiet streets and sidewalks like this one, lined with hulking trees. Jak faces me to offer her customary high five. Her pupils and irises are nearly the same color, giving her eyes a freaky, piercing quality. I high-five her in return. Her dark skin contrasts sharply with my perpetually pale complexion.

"How about this," I say. "When we're away at college, you can call me every day on your walk home and we'll chat just like we're doing now."

"But it won't be the same," Jak says.

"It'll be pretty close."

Jak is about my height, but we once compared belly buttons and hers is two inches higher—those long legs again. Still, I probably outweigh her by about fifty pounds.

"I won't be able to do *this*," she says, as she manages to playfully nudge me off the sidewalk, onto the grass, and almost into the conspicuous tree on the corner.

I recover. "Honestly," I say, "that's what I'm looking forward to the *most*: you not being able to do that."

"You love it," she says.

I probably won't miss *all* her antics when we go away to school, but I'll definitely miss her *Jak*ness—her quick draw with a joke, her oddly endearing anxieties, her energy. At least I'll always have access to her steady stream of nonsensical yet encouraging tweets: "Shane is the Mane!"

Before we part ways for home, Jak asks, "Do you think we should try to be more social before we graduate? You know, maybe go to one of these parties, drink a lot, and make poor decisions? Instead of being antisocial and hanging out by ourselves, I mean."

I consider this. "Meh," I answer.

"Yeah. That's exactly what I was thinking," Jak says. "Meh."

"HEDGEHOG, YOU'RE BEING CUTE."

"I'm only being cute because you want me to be cute, Balloon."

"So you admit it? You're being cute."

"You got me, Balloon."

"Aw, Hedgehog."

I can't take much more of this. "Seriously, guys?"

Hedgehog and Balloon continue making googly eyes at each other. Their real names are Anthony McGuinness and Brooke Nast, and they're both sophomores. Anthony is a former client of mine. I think it's safe to say that he's a satisfied customer, considering he and Brooke have been dating for six months and have these nauseating pet names for each other. Brooke goes by Balloon. I don't know how they came up with that. Anthony goes by Hedgehog. I'm assuming this is because he's the most hirsute guy I've ever met, and the hair on his head has been corralled into little gelled spikes.

"Is this too much for you?" Anthony asks, grinning.

"No, no, please, don't mind me," I insist.

We're sitting in a little lounge area at the front of the administration hallway in school. It's just a few basic chairs and a coffee table tucked into an alcove. Less like *The O.C.* and more like Ikea. Behind us is a long stucco hallway with the principal's and vice principal's offices, guidance, and the nurse, as well as the headquarters of some after-school activities such as Model UN and Student Council.

"Shane, did you check out our new Instagram?" Brooke asks. "Hedgehogandballoon, all one word."

"We figured since we're always in each other's pictures, we might as well just share an account," Anthony adds.

"That's great, guys," I say. "I'll definitely check it out." I'm never gonna check it out.

Brooke gives Hedgehog—er, Anthony—a kiss on the lips. I'm happy for them. Every once in a while I like to check up on my former clients to see how they're doing. Sometimes guys need relationship advice or a refresher course on the Galgorithm. My work is never done. Sure, that entails the stress of being on call 24/7, but to me it's worth it when I see a couple like these two.

"So there's something I wanted to ask you," Brooke says to me.

"We both want to ask you. It's coming from both of us," Anthony says.

"Yeah," I say, "I assumed that."

I remember what dire straits Anthony was in when he first came to me for advice. Totally lovesick. He had been crushing on Brooke since fifth grade but never had the courage to ask her out. Brooke is a sprite, a tiny little pixie with cherubic cheeks who flits about smiling and giggling. Anthony once told me that Brooke lights up a room, and I immediately imagined capturing her in an upside-down mason jar like a firefly.

Anthony, on the other hand, looks like the iStockphoto image for "shy guy." Average build, forgettable face, slightly slumped posture as if he doesn't want anyone to notice him, plus about two pounds of excess hair. He was a project. Now look at him—sharing an Instagram handle with an absolute sweetheart. There's no doubt about it: Hedgehog and Balloon are, in the parlance of my female peers, "totes adorbs."

"So what's up?" I say.

"What would you think if we set you up on a double date?" Brooke asks.

"Me?"

"Yeah," Anthony says. "It would be fun."

"I don't know . . ."

"We haven't even told you who we have in mind," Brooke pleads.

For a moment I see red. It's not because I'm angry. I mean I *literally* see red. In my head I have a brief flashback to the girl I dated freshman year. We met at a Kingsview football game against our bitter rival, Valley Hills. She was two years older than me and I was smitten. But it wouldn't be long before she broke my heart in half. Jak and I call her Voldemort. Not because she's evil, but because after our breakup speaking her name was too painful for me. Voldemort was a natural redhead who accented her fiery locks by wearing red nail polish and red lipstick. I can picture those lips now, grinning at me. And then telling me it was over.

I try to push that pain aside and hear what Hedgehog and Balloon have to say.

"Okay, who do you want to set me up with?"

"Tristen Kellog."

I pause. "Really?"

"Yeah," Brooke says. "I work on the paper with her, and I think you guys would be great together."

The *Kingsview Chronicle* is not exactly the *New York Times*, but it's the official paper of record/college-application padder at our school. There are recaps of varsity sporting events and editorials about the lack of two-ply toilet paper in the bathrooms, but that's about it. Brooke fancies herself an investigative reporter. I think the last story she broke was about lunch ladies skimming off the top of the fruit salad, a scandal that became known as Watermelongate.

"You guys want to set up a double date with me and Tristen Kellog?"

"Yeah," Anthony says, "what do you think?"

Tristen is the *It* girl of the junior class. Popular. Hot. If she doesn't win Most Attractive in the yearbook awards when she graduates next year, I'll come back from college to demand a recount myself. If I were a superficial guy, Tristen would be my number one. But the thing is, I don't consider myself a superficial guy. I like to think I have a little substance. A touch of class. I care about more than just popularity and appearances. Tristen and I have spoken maybe ten words to each other in all of high school. And let's just say she won't be in the running for Most Likely to Succeed. Or, for that matter, Most Likely to Spell Succeed.

"Guys," I venture diplomatically, "I really appreciate it, but I'm good."

"Are you sure?" Brooke asks.

"Just think about it," Anthony adds.

I mean, I would be crazy not to at least *think* about it. I like to date. Creating and maintaining the Galgorithm would not be possible without a lot of firsthand experience. But I prefer to initiate contact myself, to be in control—just in case. You never know if the next girl is gonna be another Voldemort.

While I contemplate this, Anthony and Brooke return to their favorite interest: each other.

"Hedgehog, there's Pinkberry in the cafeteria today. Wanna get some?"

"Awesome idea, Balloon!"

They stand up.

"Do you want anything?" Brooke asks me.

"No, thanks."

"K. Let us know if you change your mind about the Tristen thing."

"Will do."

Brooke turns to leave. Anthony lingers for a moment as he shakes my hand goodbye. He gives me the look of an eternally grateful man.

"Talk later?" he says.

"Yup."

Brooke has no idea that I played any role in them getting together. There was actually a moment in the newlywed, six-weeks-in, *let's share everything about ourselves* phase of their relationship when Anthony confided that he was considering telling Brooke about me. I scolded him. Brooke does not need to know that I stood over him and told him what to text her every day for two months like a modern-day Cyrano.

I have a few minutes to kill before my next class. It's definitely flattering that Hedgehog and Balloon want to set me up with Tristen. Sure, I wish I had even a lick of stubble on my face, and I never bother combing my mop of brown hair, but I think I'm doing all right for myself in the looks department.

The bell rings, breaking my train of thought, and soon there are swarms of students filling the halls. In the three-plus years I've spent at Kingsview High, I've managed to stay out of the silos and cliques. That's why it's not weird to see me sitting with Reed in the cafeteria one day and chatting up Hedgehog and Balloon the next. In just a few months, though, graduation will be here and everything will change.

Before I get too existential, I spot Mr. Kimbrough, my old math teacher, walking toward me with a determined look in his eyes. He seems pained. And something tells me I'm about to find out why.

5

I HAD MR. KIMBROUGH TWO YEARS ago in tenth grade. Nice guy. Nerdy enough to hold court as a math teacher but stocky enough to pass for a gym teacher. Early thirties and you can tell that he was going bald but then made a preemptive strike and just shaved his head. It suits him, unlike the sweater vests he always wears.

Since I was in his class, we've exchanged the occasional friendly nod in the halls, but that's about it. This time, though, he comes right over to me.

"Mr. Chambliss, how are you?"

"Hey, Mr. Kimbrough. I'm good."

"Do you have a moment?"

"Uh, I have to get to class."

"It'll be quick. Take a walk with me."

We head through a side door and out to a large courtyard at the front of the school. It's the first thing you see when you drive onto campus, and it looks like a brochure: small fountain, rows of well-manicured flower beds, a few palm trees, and about a dozen circular cement tables surrounded by benches. Kids are hanging out, listening to music, and eating lunch. Thankfully, no one seems to notice or care that I'm strolling around with a teacher whose class I'm not even in. A teacher who, I might add, is obsessed with math. He used to draw math-related cartoons on the backs of our quizzes and rattle off cringeworthy math jokes all the time in class. But, hey, if you know what you like, go with it.

"So how's calc, Shane?" Mr. Kimbrough asks.

I guess that's what passes for small talk in this situation.

"It's going fine. You know."

"Yeah, yeah, I know."

An awkward pause. I wish he would just cut to the chase.

"So, I know this is a little unusual, Shane, but there's something I wanted to ask you."

"Okay . . ."

"I've heard some people say that you're a bit of a Svengali when it comes to romance."

"A what?"

"Like a dating . . . mastermind of some sort."

Uh oh. Every once in a while a whisper about my exploits surfaces from Kingsview's primordial gossip ooze. I take precautions to remain discreet, but it's a daunting task against the power of a high school rumor mill. When kids start to talk, I usually tamp it down with the help of my clients, who are taught to "deny till you die." But this is the first time I've ever had an *adult* say anything about it to me.

"I have no idea what you're talking about," I respond swiftly.

"Are you sure? You're not in trouble or anything. I'm just . . . curious if you're some kind of expert or something."

"I wish, Mr. Kimbrough. But I'm definitely not."

I hope that will satisfy his curiosity, end this line of questioning, and allow me to go about my day and my life.

It does not.

"You know Adam Foster, right?" he asks.

I try not to react. Adam is a fellow senior and one of my former clients. A real doofus but a good guy. This might be a stab in the dark by Mr. Kimbrough, or maybe he knows more than he's letting on. I decide to tread lightly and see what happens. "Yeah. I know him."

"He was in my class last year," Mr. Kimbrough says. "And between me and you, he's a bit . . ." He leans in to whisper in my ear. "*Off.*"

I'm not sure Mr. Kimbrough is one to talk, but nonetheless I say, "I guess that's true."

"I started to notice you guys chatting in the halls," he says. "It almost seemed like you were . . . *advising* him. And now,

I don't know if you know this, but I heard he's dating Olivia Reyes."

Of course I know that. Olivia is a head turner. Getting her and Adam together was some of my finest work.

"And no offense to Adam," Mr. Kimbrough continues, "but Olivia is kind of, you know . . . out of his league."

One of my pet peeves is the phrase "out of your league." That's an excuse. That's what chumps say. I've had many a client fret that the girl he's after is "out of his league." I tell him never to speak those words again. If you say it, then you believe it, and then she *is* out of your league. If only Mr. Kimbrough had been born fifteen years later, I could have taught him a thing or two.

"Did you have anything to do with that?" he asks me flat-out.

"No. I had nothing to do with Adam Foster dating Olivia Reyes," I lie, just as flat-out.

Mr. Kimbrough looks deflated. I actually feel bad.

"I could have sworn," he murmurs, "that I heard someone talking about an *algorithm*."

I stop in my tracks. Mr. Kimbrough's snooping has gone deeper than I thought. I need to try more evasive maneuvers.

"Well you are a math teacher, Mr. Kimbrough," I offer. "I'm sure people talk about algorithms around you all the time."

"Yeah, but this was different."

We've reached an uncomfortable impasse in the conversation. We've also reached the stairs that lead from the courtyard to the parking lot. From here you can see the entire front of the school—all white walls with Spanish-style red clay shingles on the roof. I glance at Mr. Kimbrough. I can sense the wheels turning in his head. It's apparent that he's not gonna let this go easily. I can continue to feign ignorance and hope he doesn't ask more questions, or I can take control of the situation by trying one more thing: indulging him.

"Mr. Kimbrough, I'm no expert. And I don't know what algorithm you're talking about. But . . . maybe I can try to help anyway?"

He considers this. "I appreciate it, Shane, but this is inappropriate. I shouldn't have wasted your time."

"It's not inappropriate. We're just two guys chatting. It's okay." That said, we both look around to make sure no one is staring at us. Next period's bell has already rung and everyone is scrambling inside. I'm gonna be late. Whatever. Mr. Kimbrough has gotten my attention.

He leans in once more and speaks softy: "Do you know Ms. Solomon?"

"Sure," I say. "She teaches history." I've never been in her class, but I've seen Ms. Solomon around the halls. She's younger than Mr. Kimbrough, maybe late twenties, and kind of a fox. If she is what this is all about, then I have newfound respect for the man.

"Well . . . the thing is . . . ," he stammers.

"You're crushing on her," I say.

Mr. Kimbrough nods his head as if he's admitting this to himself for the first time. "I guess you could say that."

"Have you asked her out?" I say.

"Oh God, no!"

"Why not?"

"She's the most beautiful woman in the world," he says. "My love for her is . . . divided by zero."

"Divided by zero?"

"Undefined, Shane. Have you forgotten your algebra?"

Ah, math joke. Mr. Kimbrough, you're killing me.

"Shane, the thing is . . . Deb—er, Ms. Solomon—is such an incredible person. I wouldn't want to sully that by asking her out, like a peasant. And, oh man, what if she turned me down? I'd have to get a new job. Refinance my mortgage . . ."

"Mr. Kimbrough, slow your roll. Relax."

A classic pitfall of nerds of all ages: talking yourself into rejection before you've even done anything. I call it pre-rejection. Or just *prejection*. But at least Mr. Kimbrough has passion. I can work with passion.

"Do you know what Ms. Solomon likes?" I ask.

"Likes? Hmmm. Well, she's mentioned she enjoys teaching about the Civil War." Mr. Kimbrough ponders this further. "You know what? There's actually a Civil War exhibit at Memorial Museum this month."

"Perfect."

"I can't just *ask* her, though. What if she says no? I could never look her in the eye again."

Something makes me think that Mr. Kimbrough isn't making much eye contact with her to begin with.

"Well," I say, "is there a list of all the teachers' e-mail addresses?"

"Yeah, there is. Could I just ask her out over e-mail?"

"No, no, no. Not exactly. But here's something you *can* try. Write an e-mail to all the teachers and say that you have tickets to the Civil War exhibit. Ask if anyone wants to go. But here's the key: *Only send the e-mail to her, and put her address in the BCC.* That way it seems like you're sending a mass e-mail to everyone, but you're really only sending it to her. She'll respond because it seems like a casual group thing and not like you're asking her out. Then you're in."

The ol' BCC switcheroo. A Galgorithm classic.

Mr. Kimbrough thinks through my advice for a moment.

"Shane, that's brilliant."

"Nah. Just something I tried once. Maybe it will work for you." I attempt to play it off so that he doesn't get even more suspicious about me.

"But isn't it a little dishonest?"

What a heart of gold. I'm starting to like this guy more and more.

"Mr. Kimbrough," I say, "all you're trying to do is get in

the same room with Ms. Solomon. After that, it's up to you. There's nothing dishonest about it."

Mr. Kimbrough considers this.

"Besides," I add, "all's fair in love and Civil War."

He smiles. "You're right. I'll give it a try. And . . . if you could maybe not mention this to anyone . . ."

"As long as you do the same," I say.

"Deal."

"Good luck, Mr. Kimbrough."

"Thanks, Shane."

Crisis averted. For now.

6

I WAS A MESS AFTER Voldemort ended things. In hindsight, I had no idea what I was doing when I was with her. I didn't know how to talk. I didn't know how to act. I didn't know all the subtleties that girls expect from the guys they choose to be with.

When you date someone two years older, you have to learn a lot of lessons the hard way. For instance, everyone always says that it's what's inside that counts. And that's true. But no girl is ever going to appreciate your insides if she can't stand your outsides. No one ever told me otherwise, until it was too late.

I contemplate this cruel truth as I walk through the mall with Reed on a Saturday afternoon. Today's mission is a joint makeover/pep talk. I need to motivate him to make a move on Marisol and I also need him to look the part when he does. The mall is great for both objectives, because not only are there plenty of clothing stores catering to the gaunt teenager, but there are also tons of girls around.

Much like our high school, Kingsview Mall is open-air. The main concourses are completely uncovered, and the shops, which do have ceilings, line either side. Reed and I are in a jeans store, and I'm trying to find a pair suitable to his suddenly selective tastes.

"What about these?" I ask.

"Eh . . . too blue."

"Okay. How about these?"

"Too stiff."

"Too stiff? That's not a thing. What about these?"

"The zipper is weird."

"Reed, why do I get the feeling you're not gonna like anything I pick out?"

"Why do I need new jeans anyway? What's wrong with these?"

"Where did you get them?"

"I don't know; my mom got them for me."

"That's what's wrong with them."

"Ugh. All right. I guess I'll try some on."

"I mean, you're not even wearing a belt right now."

"I don't need a belt with these. They fit fine."

"You *always* need a belt. It ties everything together. Unless you think Marisol likes slobs. Because that's what girls think about guys who don't wear belts."

"Hmm. Marisol does not seem like the slob-liking type."

"Exactly. The thing you gotta realize, Reed, is that you're not just buying a bunch of denim stitched together. You're buying an image. Girls pay attention to the jeans you're wearing. Jeans speak to girls."

"What does that even mean?"

"Let's say you're wearing dumpy jeans. Like, just for example, the jeans you're wearing now."

"Dude!"

"I'm sorry, I'm sure your mom is a lovely woman, but she bought you dumpy jeans. And when a girl sees that, she thinks one thing: He doesn't care. And if he doesn't care about his jeans, then he doesn't care about himself. Girls want a guy who makes an effort. Who's at least mature enough to put himself together. Because if he doesn't care about himself, then how's he gonna treat me?"

Reed is standing there with his mouth agape. "All that from a pair of jeans?"

"Yes! Why do you think I always wear such clean, slim-fit, button-fly jeans?"

"Uh. I don't know. I've never looked at your crotch before."

"Well you should start."

Reed looks puzzled.

"Next up," I add, "shoes."

"Shoes?"

"Oh yeah. I want you looking your best when you ask Marisol out."

"And when is that gonna be, exactly?"

"Next week."

Reed gulps. "That's soon."

"It is. But, you know, that's what the Galgorithm says."

"I mean, I respect that and all, but how do you know that the Galgorithm is even right?"

I continue looking through the rack of jeans. This question inevitably springs up with every client.

"First of all," I say, "it's not always right. But sticking to the formula can definitely improve your chances."

"Okay, but what *is* the formula?"

"I don't think you're ready to know that yet. You just have to trust me."

"Is there a code? Is it in a spreadsheet?"

"Reed, what's your favorite sport?"

"Favorite sport . . . Does Dungeons and Dragons count as a sport?"

Really? "Right, I forgot who I'm dealing with. So, you know how in Dungeons and Dragons you move your piece to a certain square and then you follow the directions accordingly?"

"That's not exactly how it works—"

"Reed, it's an analogy!"

"Sorry. I mean, *not* sorry!"

"My point is, the Galgorithm tells you where to go at each point in the game. But you don't need to know the formula itself. Because you have me to guide you."

This seems to reassure him.

"All right. Man, I wish I knew girls like you do."

"Believe me, it's no easy task," I say. "Girls aren't like us. Their blood flows to their heart. Our blood flows to our groin."

I hear snickering from behind me. I turn to see two cute girls standing there. They must have overheard what I just said.

"My bad," I say to the girls. "You weren't supposed to hear that last part."

"No worries," the brunette says with a smirk. She looks at her friend and rolls her eyes.

The other girl, who has a nose ring, is holding a guys' belt with a price tag on it.

"Hey, if you don't mind me asking," I say, "where did you find that belt? My buddy Reed over here is looking for one."

Reed is frozen in place.

Nose Ring points. "Over there. On the other side of the display."

"Is it for your boyfriend?" I ask.

"No," she says, suddenly bashful. "It's for me. I just like guys' belts. Is that weird?"

"I don't know. Reed, what do you think? Is it weird?"

Reed is a deer caught in headlights. He goes mute.

"Is your friend okay?" the brunette asks.

"Yes," Reed interjects at last. "It's weird."

Nose Ring is taken aback. "Really?"

"Well," Reed says haltingly, "only because the buckle doesn't go with your nose ring. One's gold; the other is silver."

Nose Ring starts to nod her head. "Weird. But you're right. Good call."

Reed manages a shrug.

"Let's go put this back," Nose Ring says to the brunette. "Thanks," she says to Reed.

"Okay," the brunette says. Then, to Reed and me: "Nice to meet you guys."

The two girls blush, smile, and walk away.

When they're out of earshot, Reed exhales and says to me, "Dude, what just happened?"

"What just happened was your first field test. We flirted with them and you did great!"

"I think I blacked out. I don't even know what I did."

"We just followed the rules," I say. "*Be different*: I accidentally got their attention with that off-color remark. Then, instead of going the easy route and saying the belt was fine, you *noticed* it didn't match her nose ring. And, finally, you *told* her to her face in a polite manner. Be different. Notice her. Tell her. Just like I always say."

Reed contemplates this for a moment and then pulls out his notebook and starts scribbling furiously. "Noted!" He has a huge grin on his face. "Shane, I want you to pick out anything in this whole mall and I will buy it! I am on board. I will do anything you say. Your wish is my command. Let's get some jeans!"

Finally he's starting to get it.

7

"YOUR PARENTS GO OUT OF TOWN for the night and this is what we do?" Jak says.

I'm lying next to Jak in a hammock in my backyard. The yard is disproportionately large compared to my parents' modest split-level house, but the hammock is the only thing out here. There's no patio, no pool. The hammock isn't even tied to two trees; it's just held up by a freestanding base smack-dab in the middle of the lawn.

"What should we have done instead?" I ask. "Have a party?"

"Yes. In fact, that's a great idea. Why don't we have a party?"

"Jak, is there really anyone you would rather hang out with than me?"

"I can think of *tons* of people."

"Okay. Name one."

The night is quiet and beautiful.

"I'm still waiting," I say.

"I'm still thinking!"

I cross my arms.

"Fine," she says. "You're right. I hate everyone else."

"See. I knew that. That's why I didn't invite anyone over. I'm a great best friend."

"Yeah," Jak admits, "you're pretty good."

On a weekend night like tonight I'm usually running around town with a client, coaching him or helping him scout a crush. On slower nights, which have been fewer and farther between lately, I hang out with Jak. We go through the motions of picking a destination—movies, bowling alley, mall—before inevitably ending up in this hammock, staring up at the stars, and BSing for hours. That way Jak doesn't have to deal with the social anxiety she so clearly suffers from.

Tall cedars on three sides separate my yard from the neighbors, so it's actually pretty private back here. The late January air is cool, but I wouldn't change a thing. It's really peaceful. Usually I'm fidgety and can't sit still for more than a few minutes. But I couldn't be more content than to hang right here with Jak all night. Soon, though, she breaks the silence:

"Do you think your parents have had sex in this hammock?"

"Oh, goddamn it, Jak! That's gross!"

This is one of Jak's things: She prides herself on ruining perfect moments with an inappropriate comment. She says perfect moments make her feel uncomfortable. After all these years I still never see it coming.

"What?" she asks coyly. "I just want to know if your mom and dad, who gave birth to you and raised you, have had sexual intercourse in the very spot where we're currently lying. What's the big deal?"

I stick my fingers in my ears. "La-la-la-la-la I can't hear you!"

Jak tickles me. I have to pull my fingers out of my ears to defend myself.

"Get off!" I gasp.

We laugh our faces blue and almost fall out of the hammock.

"Sorry about that," Jak says. "The moment was just too good. Had to ruin it."

"It's fine," I say.

"Hey, guess who I saw this week making out in the middle of the hallway," Jak says. "Anthony McGuinness and Brooke Nast."

"You know, for someone who claims to hate everyone, you sure are pretty nosy."

"Whatever."

"What do you care about Hedgehog and Balloon?" I ask.

"Whohog and what now?"

"Hedgehog and Balloon. That's what Anthony and Brooke call each other."

"Hedgehog and Balloon sounds like a Japanese power-pop band."

"Jak, that is the weirdest observation ever. Also: I totally agree."

"See? I'm good."

"You know, I actually meant to tell you—Anthony and Brooke want to set me up on a double date."

"Intriguing," Jak says. "With *whom?*"

"Whom" is Jak's favorite word. She stresses it every chance she gets. Another one of her bizarre idiosyncrasies.

"Tristen Kellog."

"Wow. She's pretty."

I trust Jak's opinion on girls more than anyone's, but I was wary about bringing up Tristen. I've been warming to the idea of us going out, but I thought Jak might disapprove.

"So . . . you're into the idea?" I ask.

"Yeah. She seems nice, I guess. I wish I had her boobs."

"I don't know," I say. "She's kinda boring."

"Um, you're not gonna have sex with her *demeanor.*"

I laugh. Jak has a way with words.

"Maybe," she continues, "you could hook up with her right here on this hammock, where your parents conceived you."

"Jak!"

"Just sayin'."

"So you don't think it's a bad idea if I go on a double date with her?"

"Not at all."

It's settled then. With Jak's seal of approval I'm gonna do it.

"Tristen Kellog?" she continues. "Bravo, Chambliss. You've come a long way from oversize baggy jeans and a pocket protector."

"I never had a pocket protector! It was a piece of cardboard that came with the shirt."

"But you didn't take it out of the pocket."

I sigh happily. There's no way to stop Jak when she starts in on me. I just have to roll with it. (But I swear it was a piece of cardboard.)

"You're lucky they want to set you up," Jak adds. "No one is trying to set *me* up."

Jak is single, and perpetually so, possibly because of her uncanny ability to discover every guy's flaws.

"I can try to set you up, if you want."

"You're only saying that because you know I hate everyone and will never take you up on it."

"Yeah, you're right," I admit. "But seriously, guys talk. If you ever wanted a date at school, believe me, you wouldn't have a problem."

"Really? What do guys say about me? Is it locker room talk? Are your penises out?"

"I never should have mentioned it."

She smiles. "It's nice to hear, Shane. Thanks."

Jak is there for me and I'm there for her. She was my

shoulder to cry on when things went sideways with Voldemort. But even with her help, it took me a long time to recover. Nothing was ever the same after that experience. Voldemort really did a number on me. So I decided never to let that pain of heartbreak happen again—not to me, not to anyone—as much as I could help it. Maybe it was a naive mission, to become an expert on girls, but I needed something to focus my energy on.

Truth is, even though I haven't spoken to Voldemort in years and she has long since gone away to college, I'm still tender. I never got a real explanation for why we broke up. I've dated other girls, but my heart isn't in it because I'm too afraid to have it shattered again. Jak has been encouraging me to get back out there in a real way, but I've busied myself with my clients' love lives instead.

Maybe it's about time I stopped making excuses and started walking the walk.

8

THESE DAYS IT SEEMS like there's a college fair after school every week. I don't have any practical use for them, of course, and plan on beginning my slow slide into senioritis any day now. But when the final class period bell rings, my duties as a dating guru are only just beginning. Events like these are a good opportunity to mingle with clients, potential clients, and some of their lovely female would-be companions. This afternoon is particularly important because the time has come for Reed to ask Marisol out.

The stage in the school auditorium is packed with booths from different colleges and universities, each manned by an eager undergrad. There are more booths on the floor in front of the stage, and then there are rows of fold-down theater seats where I'm currently standing, waiting for Reed.

I spot Adam Foster and Olivia Reyes a few rows behind me and notice that their body language does not look good. This was the couple that Mr. Kimbrough found so unbelievable that he (rightfully) assumed I had something to do with them getting together. I make a mental note to check in with Adam.

A little closer to the stage, Marisol is chatting with Rebecca Larabie, the school president, who Jak heard through the grapevine had recently hooked up with Harrison. I assume she and Marisol know each other because Marisol is also on student government as junior-class treasurer. Marisol looks like she's in a good mood, which is not always readily evident because her eyebrows naturally arch like a telenovela villain's. This is great news for Reed.

Finally the man himself arrives in a tizzy.

"I'm only five minutes late," Reed says, a bit flustered. "And I'm not sorry."

I smile. Reed is proving to be a model pupil. I imagine he spent the morning before school primping and prepping for hours in front of a mirror, getting ready for this moment. I sniff him.

"Perfect amount of cologne," I observe.

"I did what you said. I sprayed it away from me and then just walked through the cloud once."

"Excellent," I say. "You smell good. But not *too* good."

I give Reed a once-over. Look, he's still a nerd. But the plan isn't to turn him into something he's not. It's to turn him into the best version of himself. To make him feel like he can take on the world. And with new jeans, a decent haircut, and a T-shirt that actually fits him instead of drooping off his bony shoulders like it's still on the hanger, I think we did pretty well.

"Nice belt," I say with a smirk.

"Is Marisol here?" Reed asks.

"There. Next to Rebecca."

We both glance over at them from a distance. Marisol is gregarious and comfortable in her own skin. Everything Reed wishes he could be. He lets out a long sigh, like all the confidence just left his body.

"Reed, you got this. I promise. Just remember everything we've talked about the past few weeks. Trust the Galgorithm."

He steels himself. "Okay. What's our point of entry?"

"I'm gonna run a wedge to remove Rebecca from the equation. Once she's separated, all you have to do is swoop in and engage with Marisol."

Reed starts paging through his little notebook. "Wedge, wedge, where is that . . ."

I put my hand out to stop him. "Reed. I'm just gonna go talk to Rebecca and wedge her out of the way. Not everything is rocket science."

"Right. Noted."

"Are you ready?"

He nods, still grasping the notebook.

"Good. Now put that thing away and follow me fifteen seconds behind. Too soon and it will be obvious. Too late and Marisol will drift away."

"Got it."

Satisfied that Reed is up to the challenge, I pat him on the shoulder and then leave to approach Rebecca. But when I'm about twenty feet away, I realize that I'm not the only one seeking her attention. Harrison has arrived in the auditorium and made it over to her first.

Harrison looks like a 1950s football star with his square jaw and blond crew cut. He's about six feet tall with zero body fat and knuckles that apparently need constant cracking—when they're not dragging on the floor, that is. He and I have a checkered history. At a mutual friend's bar mitzvah back in the day, we almost came to blows when he thought I was eyeing a girl he was interested in. Never mind that I never even looked at the girl in question and was merely eyeing the bathroom after an unusually long haftarah. The rabbi intervened, but I'm pretty sure Harrison has kept me on an enemies list taped next to his bed ever since.

Harrison and Rebecca hooking up is not public knowledge and has been denied by both parties, but their eye contact tells me it's on like Donkey Kong. Besides, there's no reason why Harrison would show his face at a college fair other than to see Rebecca. He already has a baseball scholarship and will be sparking bench-clearing brawls in D-1 come next season.

Knowing Reed is following my lead, I continue forward anyway.

"Hey, Rebecca!" I say as I reach her.

She smiles pleasantly. "Hi, Shane."

I acknowledge Harrison with a nod but pretend I don't even see Marisol and focus all my attention on Rebecca. She has curly brown hair that frames her oval face and is prepped out in J.Crew everything. She and I have been reasonably friendly since middle school.

"What's going on with the senior parking lot permits?" I ask. This was one of Rebecca's major campaign issues, and I know she is champing at the bit to discuss the mind-numbing minutiae of the problem with anyone who will listen.

Indeed, she lights ups. "You know what? I *just* had a meeting with the administration about that yesterday. The issue is . . ."

I can sense Harrison growing impatient, but I do my best to avoid looking at him. As Rebecca continues talking, I slyly position myself between her and Marisol, with my back to Marisol, effectively cutting her off from both Rebecca and Harrison.

Classic wedge. Separation achieved.

"Another part of the problem," Rebecca says to me, "is a lack of data and analytics about traffic flow in the parking lot. What we need . . ."

Now I'm counting in my head: . . . *ten Mississippi, eleven Mississippi, twelve Mississippi*. When I hit fifteen, I hear Reed sidle up to Marisol behind me like clockwork. I continue talking to Rebecca, but am much more interested in overhearing Reed.

"Hey, Marisol."

"Oh, hey, Reed."

She remembers his name. Small victories.

"I can't believe there's *another* college fair. School is ending so fast!" Reed says.

(Common interests.)

"I know, right? Crazy," she says.

"What do you think about staying in-state versus going away?" Reed asks.

(Open-ended question.)

"Oh, I'm trying to get the heck out of here. What about you?" Marisol replies.

(Agree with whatever the hell she says.)

"Totally. Me too. I want to get as far away from Kingsview as possible."

"Nice," she says.

Nice! I think. You got this, Reed!

"So, any big plans for the weekend?" he asks.

"Uh, not really sure. Probably just hanging out."

There's a brief pause where I think Reed has panicked and lost his nerve. Meanwhile, Rebecca is droning on about parking regulations in my other ear and Harrison is glaring at me.

"There's that new pizza place on Hickory," Reed says finally. "You wanna maybe check it out on Friday night?"

Marisol is caught off guard. She loves pizza. Her Facebook profile is littered with photos and memes about it, including a post about the new joint in town. Reed has been under strict orders *not* to like or comment on any of them. You must be a ninja and observe silently.

"You mean . . . like a date?" she asks.

I tell all my clients: If you are ever in the very enviable position where a girl is asking you to clarify whether it's a date or not, always say, *Yes, it's a date.* Most guys take this opportunity to hedge rejection, to play it cool, to keep things open. Wrong.

Come on, Reed. Remember your training. Close the deal.

"Yeah, like a date," he says.

How many times has Marisol ever been asked out so directly? She's probably flattered.

"Sure," she says. "That'd be fun."

I pump my fist. Rebecca looks at me like I have three heads. I do not care. Harrison fumes. Just a few seconds longer . . .

"Awesome," Reed says. "I'll message you."

Most guys ask for her number here. Nonsense. If you're already friends on Facebook or some other social media, you can always reach out later to get her digits. Quit while you're ahead and exit before she changes her mind.

"Sounds good," Marisol says.

Get out of there, Reed!

"Cool. Well I really need to pee. I'll talk to you later."

Okay, so he didn't quite stick the landing. But I'll take it.

"Oh. All right," Marisol says.

I feel Reed breeze past me and out of the conversation.

We did it.

He did it.

9

MY DAD LIKES TO USE the phrase "We all put our pants on one leg at a time." I've begun to dole out this advice to my clients as well, in order to remind them that the seemingly ungettable girl they are pining after is really no different from them. I'm currently trying to take my own advice. I know that Tristen Kellog, the very attractive girl seated across from me, puts her pants on one leg at a time. The only problem is, they are really tight pants, and I'm having trouble paying attention.

The double date with Anthony, Brooke, and Tristen has been going pretty well so far. We're at Perkin's Beanery, a trendy, hipsterish coffee shop with artisanal ice cubes and 20 percent higher prices than Starbucks.

Tristen's aforementioned pants are painted on, and she's wearing a casual gray V-neck that offers the superficial man just a peek at her incredible cleavage. Her face is perfectly symmetrical save for two little moles on her left check. Her hair is straw-colored and her eyes are cartoonishly blue. I don't think Anthony has ever been within spitting distance of a girl as gorgeous as Tristen, and despite his unconditional love for Brooke, he has clammed up in the corner of our table.

"Hedgehog, are you feeling okay? You're so quiet," Brooke asks.

Anthony glances at Tristen, looks at me knowingly, and then rests his head on Brooke's shoulder.

"Don't worry, Balloon will take care of you," Brooke says, as she strokes his face.

"Aren't they cute?" Tristen asks me.

"I have to admit, they are pretty cute," I say. "How's your coffee?"

"Pretty good. Thanks again for treating. They didn't have any almond milk or soy milk, so I just got nonfat."

"What *is* almond milk anyway?"

"It's milk from ground-up almonds. It's healthier because there's no dairy."

"That feels like one of those made-up facts."

"No, it's true!" she says. "I heard it somewhere. Either Oprah or Twitter. I can't remember."

"Right. Well, cheers."

Tristen and I clink our coffee cups together. She takes a sip and smiles. She has a great smile. Very disarming. Tristen is a pretty face, no doubt. But I'm hard-pressed to figure out if there's anything beneath the surface. I know I'm being picky, but ever since Voldemort I've treaded carefully, terrified that I might go too far down the path with the wrong girl and have things end badly. All I'm asking for is a dose of personality from Tristen, who must be as bored as I am, because she's tapping her nails on the table. Her nail polish is pink, and each ring finger also sports a yellow smiley face. I hate the fact that I know this is called an "accent nail."

Suddenly, Brooke perks up. She has been cooing with Anthony but apparently realizes she may have to better involve herself. "Hey, Tristen, tell Shane what you're doing this summer."

I'm imagining a sleepaway camp dedicated to spray tanning.

"I'm leading a Habitat for Humanity trip to the Midwest," Tristen says. "We're gonna build homes for families that lost them in all those tornadoes."

"What?" I stammer, and almost spit up some nine-dollar iced coffee.

"Unfortunately," she continues, "there are more than five million households in America that are in desperate need of new housing."

"I didn't know that," I say, attempting to recover. "Is that from Oprah or Twitter?"

"The US Department of Housing and Urban Development."

"Oh."

"It's just something I feel strongly about," Tristen says. "We've, like, got it so good in Kingsview. I just think we should help other people out. Plus it's an opportunity to really get my hands dirty."

I'm stunned. I try to imagine Tristen's accent nails digging into dirt and making habitats for humanity. Apparently there *is* another side to her.

"That's really cool," I say, trying to keep the conversation going. "So, Brooke, you guys met at the *Chronicle*, right?"

"Yup," Brooke says.

"I really liked that fruit salad exposé, by the way," I add.

"Aw, thanks."

Now I'm just buttering up everybody.

"Do you do investigative journalism, too?" I ask Tristen.

"No, I have a fashion column. Have you read it?"

"Uh, no, I don't think so."

"My latest piece is called 'Jeggings: Miracle or Disaster?'"

"Okay . . ."

"I'm also doing an article on the most blinged-out celebrity iPhone cases."

Tristen is apparently a Renaissance woman—part humanitarian, part fashionista. It's not what I expected at all, and it's intriguing. I glance over at Anthony and Brooke, who are now rubbing their noses together and whispering sweet nothings into each other's ears. They are truly the perfect couple. And I helped make it happen. Yet Tristen still has me thrown.

The last thing I need is a repeat of Voldemort and the events of freshman year. But Tristen seems worth the risk. I decide I want to go on another date with her, this time sans Hedgehog and Balloon. The only thing left to figure out is how to make it happen. Double-date-to-solo-date conversion is not an easy maneuver. We've been at Perkin's for a while now, and I can sense the end of the date looming. I imagine what one of my clients would do if he were in a similar situation. Then I realize that most of my clients are slack-jawed mathletes who have trouble stringing together two sentences in front of a girl. Don't get me wrong, I've dedicated my life to helping the poor schmoes, but they would be nowhere without me as a fail-safe.

It's getting late: Groupthink kicks in, and we all get up from the table at the same time. And then it hits me: *fail-safe*.

I know exactly what to do.

"Hey," I say to Tristen, before she can make for the exit. "Your eyelashes are really pretty. And long, too."

Tristen pauses and instinctively bats her eyes. "OMG. *Thank you*. No one has ever said that to me before. You're so sweet."

She smiles. A *big* smile. I'll wait for Hedgehog and Balloon to walk ahead of us before I ask Tristen for another date, but I already know: I'm golden.

10

I JUST FINISHED MY FINAL period—Spanish—and I'm walking through school to meet Jak out in the courtyard when I hear a familiar voice calling *mi nombre*.

"Mr. Chambliss!"

It's Mr. Kimbrough, hustling down the hall to get my attention. He's barely exerted himself, yet he's already perspiring through his sweater vest. I give him a break, pause, and let him catch up.

"Shane, I need to talk to you."

"What's going on, Mr. K.?" I'm attempting some measure of nonchalance here in this hallway full of my peers.

"I have to talk to you about . . . *Deb*," he whispers.

"Who?"

"You know . . ."

"Oh," I say. "Ms. Solomon." I almost forgot.

Mr. Kimbrough puts his finger on his lips. "*Shhhh!* Can we talk in a classroom?"

"Mr. Kimbrough, I don't know what you want from me."

"Look, Shane, what you suggested worked! I e-mailed Deb and we went to the museum together. It was amazing! But I don't know what to do next. And I know this is weird, but I have a feeling that somehow you just *get it*. I could really use some more help."

Something begins to tickle my nostrils and then the top of my esophagus. I try to clear my throat. Then I start to cough.

"Shane, are you okay?"

"Is that your . . . cologne?"

"Oh, yeah. I just got it at the mall. The woman behind the counter said it's their most popular one."

"No, Mr. K., that's the *last* one you should get. You want to be different, not the same. How much did you put on?" I cough again.

"I don't know. A few spritzes. On each wrist. And my neck."

I rub my eyes.

"No? No good?" Mr. Kimbrough says. "Is there a brand you like better?"

"I should probably go," I say.

But Mr. Kimbrough is having none of it. "Shane, I can't stop thinking about her. She's so smart. And talented. And *funny*. But she's a ten. And I'm a four. If I could just even out that fraction a little bit, we could be one."

I stare at Mr. Kimbrough. "What? Do you have these lines preplanned?"

"Five minutes is all I ask, Shane."

I look at Mr. Kimbrough and see lots of potential but very little confidence. An ideal client for the Galgorithm—other than, you know, the fact that he's a grown man. I pity him, but I also envy him. He's in love. Straight-up, head-over-heels, bad-fraction-pun love. I recall fondly the days before I was scarred and wounded by Voldemort. Mr. K. still has hope, and it's a beautiful thing.

"Fine," I say. "Five minutes."

Mr. Kimbrough breathes a sigh of gratitude.

Meanwhile, Jak is already in the courtyard stream-of-consciousness texting me, as she does every day from morning to night. I figure she'll give me five minutes before she gets tired of waiting and her texts devolve into emojis of devils and pieces of poop.

Mr. K. and I duck into an empty classroom. Paper cutouts of every U.S. president's head line the walls, remnants of a class project. These are some ugly-looking dudes. I imagine an ancestor of mine coaching these guys on how to flirt via telegram.

Mr. K. closes the door and leans against the teacher's desk. Ironic, since he's fast becoming my student.

"So," I say, "how was the Civil War exhibit? Romantic?"

"It was incredible. She loved it. I mean, it was a little awkward at first, because she assumed other people were coming. But once we got that out of the way, we spent like two hours together just walking around and talking. Did you know that nearly a dozen Union army dogs died at Gettysburg?"

"No kidding. So it *was* romantic."

"I know. And that's not even the best part. After we finished walking around, she said she was hungry, so we got a bite to eat in the cafeteria."

"Mr. K., that's great! You're killin' it. You don't need me."

"Yeah, but here's the thing. After we paid, I went—"

"Wait, what do you mean, after *we* paid?"

"I offered to pay, but she insisted on splitting it."

I slap my forehead.

"Shane, I'm not an idiot. I offered to pay. She *insisted*."

"I don't care if she tried to arm-wrestle you. Never, *ever* let the girl pay. No matter what, you always pay on the first date."

"Okay, I screwed up."

"You should also pay on the second date and the third date, at the very least."

"Why?"

"Because it's the right thing to do. Because it's chivalrous. Because the girl is worth it."

Mr. Kimbrough absorbs this. I can't help but regret that no one told *me* to always pay for Voldemort.

"But even if I do pay," Mr. Kimbrough says, "how do I *get* that second date?"

"You mean you didn't ask her out again at the end of the first date? That's the optimal window right there."

"It just kind of . . . ended. I don't even think she thought it was a date."

I shake my head. "I need some time to think about it."

"Thank you, Shane."

"But there's something you can try in the meantime. If you want."

"For Deb, I'll try anything," he says.

"Good. Let me ask you this—is there a time of day or time of week when Deb is always in a good mood?"

Mr. Kimbrough contemplates this. "Well, off the top of my head, I'd say every other Thursday. That's when we get our paychecks. She doesn't get direct deposit. She just loves payday."

"Perfect. Then here's your job: Wherever she is every other Thursday when she gets that check, you should be near her. Teachers' lounge, front office, wherever."

"Okay. I can do that. Why?"

"I know you don't teach biology, but remember Pavlov? Whenever Deb gets good news, I want you to be close by. Eventually, she'll associate you with good news."

"Shane, that can't possibly work."

"Fine, you don't want my help? I tried."

"No, no, no, no, no. I'll do it. I swear. I promise. I'm sorry."

I almost give him the "stop apologizing" speech but decide against it. I'm in a bit of an odd situation, because I've convinced Mr. K. that I'm *not* an expert, yet I'm still doling out advice. Hopefully, he won't get suspicious again. As it is I'm on shaky ground: Although I've made it my mission to help high school guys find love, I've never helped a high school *teacher* before. Who knows if my methods will even work on adults?

My worry, however, is interrupted by the constant vibrating of my phone. I'm now officially late, which means I'm on the receiving end of a barrage of emoji poop courtesy of Jak.

11

JAK IS PISSED AT ME. I can tell because she's running as fast as possible to get away from me. Unfortunately for her, we're both on treadmills and she can't get far.

The plan was to meet up after school and then go to the gym. She only waited a few minutes before deciding that I had abandoned her, and headed on without me. The odd thing is that in all our years of friendship, we've never once worked out together. The only time I've ever lifted a weight was when it was mandatory in phys ed; Jak has the rapid-fire metabolism of an adolescent cheetah and finds the idea of voluntary exercise offensive. But then she got us Fitbits and signed us up for free passes at this gym. She's either bored or having a midlife crisis at seventeen.

Sweat Republic, however, is more than just a gym, an

assumption I gather from the banners covering half the wall space, which read MORE THAN JUST A GYM. It's a New Agey Equinox meets yoga studio meets smoothie bar. Everything is painted neon and the dumbbells are arranged by "mood" instead of weight. The dozen or so other gym goers seem to be moms and dads with too much time and money on their hands. When I walked in, I found Jak still in street clothes on one of only two treadmills, which have been unceremoniously stuffed in the corner like artifacts in a museum of Dark Age fitness.

I'm now jogging alongside Jak as she gives me the silent treatment.

"Jak, I was a little late. Gimme a break."

She turns up the speed on her treadmill. So do I.

"What, did you wait like three minutes?" I ask. "At least give me a grace period."

She turns down the speed on her treadmill. So do I.

I'm annoyed, apologetic, and also a little amused.

"Where were you?" she asks finally.

"I got held up in Spanish." I don't want to bother getting into the whole Mr. Kimbrough saga.

Jak slows her treadmill down even more, to walking speed. I do the same.

"Held up in Spanish?" Jak says. *"¿Lo siento?"*

"Are you saying you're sorry? Because I'm saying *I'm* sorry."

"*¿La biblioteca es en el diablo?*"

"The library is in the devil?"

Jak takes French but knows about twenty words in Spanish that she sometimes spouts to me at random.

"You seem to be *muy* busy lately."

That time she actually used one right.

"It's my bad," I say. "I didn't mean to leave you hanging."

She checks her Fitbit. "Boom! Ten thousand steps! I win, sucka."

And with that, it's as if our little tiff never even happened.

We continue walking side by side. It feels kind of like our walks home from school together, except we're indoors and EDM is blasting in the background. The treadmills also face a mirrored wall, so I'm staring at my reflection. At five foot nine I can approach most girls even when they're in heels. My eyes are hazel; my nose is straight and thin.

Jak catches me looking at myself. "Like what you see?"

"I mean, the treadmills are going *into* the mirror," I say. "Where do you want me to look?"

Jak shrugs. She's wearing a beat-up Aerosmith T-shirt. I'm wearing an Abercrombie button-down. We're probably gonna get kicked out of here for our lack of appropriate workout attire.

"So how was your day?" I ask.

"Fine. Another day, another dollar. We had a pop quiz in history, which was *awesome*."

"That sucks. Wait, you have Ms. Solomon, right?"

"Yeah, why?"

I didn't even think about this until now, but Jak is in Deb's class. "No reason."

"She's really cute," Jak says. "But kind of a pain. I totally wanna be just like her when I grow up."

"Jak, you're *already* like that."

Jak smiles. "Aw, shucks, Chambliss. Aren't you the sweetest?" Then she reaches across the treadmills and punches me really hard in the arm.

"Ah! Goddamn it. That hurt! Why are you so bony?"

"It's a gift."

"Some gift." I rub my shoulder.

"Are you two enjoying your sweat?"

Our banter is interrupted by an overcaffeinated Sweat Republic employee. "My name is Sarah with an *h*, and I just wanted to see how your complimentary visit was going. Sweat-tastic, I hope!"

"Sure," Jak says, amused. "I'd say reasonably to quite sweat-tastic."

"Awesome!" says Sarah with an *h*. And then she starts her sales pitch: "As you may know, we have a variety of plans to fit your specific needs. Do you think you two would be interested in . . . a couple's plan? A family plan?" She kind of trails off at the end.

Jak and I glance at each other and smile. This is not the

first time someone has mistaken us for a couple, or even black and white siblings.

Sarah with an *h* realizes she may have misspoken. "None of the above?" she offers.

"We need to think about it," I say.

"Okay, great! Take all the time you need. I'm Sarah with—"

"An *h*. Yeah we got it," Jak says. I stifle a laugh.

"Right. I'll be by the front desk if you need me. Have a sweat-tastic day!"

And with that she scrams.

I turn to Jak. "Are you thinking what I'm thinking?"

"That that was the single greatest moment of my entire life?"

"Exactly."

We high-five.

My iPhone pings and I take it out of my jeans pocket. Text message.

"Give me three tries to guess who it is," Jak says.

"Deal."

"The pope."

"I would never give him my number."

"JD Salinger."

"He's dead."

"Tristen."

"Bingo. Pretty good."

Tristen and I haven't gone out again yet since our double date, but we've struck up quite the torrid text affair. I try my best to be witty and make her LOL. She sends me pleas for donations to global crises, along with occasional pictures of her nail polish. It's entertaining.

"So you and Tristen, huh?" Jak says. "Your relationship has gotten quite . . . textual."

"Oh, it's very textual."

"Are there lots of *p*'s and *v*'s?"

"Oh yeah. The *p*'s are going into the *v*'s."

"Nice," Jak says. "I want to know what her boobs are like when you touch them."

"When? You mean if."

"I mean when."

"You know I don't kiss and tell," I say.

"Who said anything about kissing? I'm talking about boob touching. Is 'don't boob-touch and tell' a thing?"

Jak is such a character. And a trouper. When Voldemort ripped out my heart like the bad guy in *Indiana Jones and the Temple of Doom* (yes, I need two movie references to explain how awful it was), Jak listened to me wail about it forever. In fact, I was in such bad shape Jak swore to me that she and I would never date. If we ever broke up, it would be devastating: Not only would I be a mess, but it would be her fault *and* she wouldn't be there to help me through it.

"When are you guys going out again?" Jak asks.

I look at my phone. "That's what I'm texting her to find out."

"What's she saying?"

"She wants to know if I'm aware of the situation in the Congo."

"What's the situation in the Congo?"

"I don't know. The next text is a dolphin emoji."

"Oh no!" Jak says. "Are dolphins being slaughtered in the Congo?"

"I don't think there *are* any dolphins in the Congo."

"Well, duh. They've all been slaughtered. That's why we need to send money."

I shake my head. "I'll get right on that."

"I wish I was in a textual relationship," Jak says.

"Is that not what we're in?" I show her my phone. "I have a hundred and twenty-three unread texts from you just from today."

"Exactly. Unread. I have needs, Shane."

"You know I have terrible service in school. But anyway, we'll work on finding you a textual partner and we'll google dolphins in the Congo. As if I didn't have enough homework from Spanish."

Jak looks at me mock-longingly and spouts three more random Spanish words: *"Amor y cacahuetes."*

"Love and peanuts?" I ask.

Jak nods. "Love and peanuts."

12

SOMETIMES DUTY CALLS at ten p.m. on a Wednesday night.

I'm driving out to the beach at this late hour to meet Adam Foster. After I noticed that something was off between him and Olivia at the college fair, I texted him a few times to check in, but he never wrote back.

Most of my successful clients, like Hedgehog, are super grateful, and keep in touch throughout the course of their relationships. But occasionally a guy finds that I remind him too much of his loveless past, or he gets caught up in his new girlfriend, and stops talking to me altogether. I assumed that was the case with Adam and didn't take it personally.

However, after not responding to my texts for a week, Adam finally replied and asked if we could meet at the beach as soon as possible. Unfortunately, my first instinct at the college fair was correct: Adam and Olivia were indeed going through a rocky patch, and they subsequently broke up.

The beach is a thirty-minute straight shot from my house. I park my silver Jeep and find Adam about halfway down to the edge of the ocean. It's really cold this close to the water, especially at night, and I'm bundled up in a too-thin Windbreaker. Except for the moon bouncing off the Pacific Ocean and the glow of Adam's phone, there's almost no light.

"Hey, buddy, how you holding up?" I say, as I sit down next to him.

There's no towel. He's just sitting directly on the sand. And he's crying.

"Terrible," he sobs. "It's over."

"What happened?"

"Olivia cheated on me. That's what happened."

"Oh man. I'm sorry."

"She was all distant," he says. "And it was like that for weeks and I didn't know why. And then finally I confronted her about it. She said she met some other guy. A friend of her brother's. I don't even know. She ended it." He has trouble continuing.

"Just take a deep breath," I say.

"*She* ended it, Shane. *She* said it was over. When you get cheated on, aren't *you* the one who's supposed to break up with the cheater? What does the Galgorithm say about *that*?"

Despite the cheap shot, I feel terrible. I pat him on the shoulder. "It's her loss. Screw her. She doesn't deserve you anyway. I'll help you meet someone who appreciates you."

"But she was the best thing that ever happened to me. How am *I* supposed to meet anyone else?"

Adam was an interesting case. He's not that bad-looking. He's over six feet tall, which is always a huge plus with the ladies. His hair is black and the consistency of a Brillo pad, but it's manageable as long as he keeps it short. His nose is big and obscures the rest of his features like an eclipse with nostrils, but I convinced him to ditch his contact lenses and pick out some cool black glasses from Warby Parker to frame his face. It totally changed his whole aura. We joke that I Clark Kented him.

Right now those glasses are coated with water droplets—a combination of tears and mist from the ocean.

"I just don't know what to do," he says.

In my line of work, there are no money-back guarantees, because there's no money involved. These are people, not vacuum cleaners. But when a client suffers a breakup, I do my best to get him back on his feet.

"Adam, I will do whatever I can. But I think if you really want to get over Olivia, you should move on as quickly as possible."

"Fine. But I don't want anyone too thin. Girls are too thin these days. It's weird."

"Not too thin. Got it."

"And no one who says 'hella.' I hate that. What does that even mean?"

"No 'hella.' Done."

This was one of Adam's major issues when I first helped him: He's the most finicky guy I've ever met. He nitpicked everyone and everything. Girls were "too nice." The air was "too breathable." He once said that a sandwich was "too bready," which I think pretty much defies the laws of sand-wichness. Adam was hopeless when he came to me: Olivia is a total free spirit, and so, by conventional standards, she and Adam were polar opposites. But much like I did with his nose and those glasses, I helped Adam frame his weakness as a positive. He's reliable, organized, and steady—voilà: just the grounding presence Olivia never even knew she needed but soon couldn't live without.

The problem with free spirits both male and female, how-ever, is that they can never truly be tamed . . . and then one day they stray.

"I can't believe she cheated on me," he says. "I did every-thing right."

"I know, man. It sucks. But unfortunately, it happens. So why don't we get back to basics. You know the drill. *Be differ-ent. Notice her. Tell her.* Let's talk about how we're gonna get you out of this rut."

"Here's the thing." He pouts. "I'm busy. I have chess

club Monday. Model UN Tuesday. Mathletes Thursday. I missed anime club today because of this whole mess."

God knows what happens if you miss anime club.

"I'm busy," he repeats. "I need someone who understands how busy I am." He starts to cry once more.

Having been the victim of epic heartbreak myself, I know that he is more than entitled to whine and sob all he wants. "It's okay, Adam. We'll find you someone who gets you and makes time for you."

I let him blubber a bit more until he finally composes himself. I pull out some tissues from the pocket of my Windbreaker and he blows his nose. I know Adam will come around to my thinking. He'll listen. He always does.

"Here's what I want you to do," I say. "Start to consider if there's anyone at school you might be interested in. If there's a bright side to this, it's that girls feel bad for a guy with a broken heart. You just got out of a relationship that ended through no fault of your own. I mean, you're a hot commodity!"

"I am?"

"Oh yeah. Sympathy is a major aphrodisiac. I know you don't trust the Galgorithm right now, but the week or two after a breakup is a great window."

"I just don't know if I'm ready."

"Adam, there's no better way to get over an ex than to meet someone new. That's just science."

"Huh. Well . . . there is *one* girl I've kinda had a crush on."

I sense an opportunity to really build up his confidence and seize it. "That's great. And guess what? You don't even need me."

"Really?"

"Yeah. Adam, you were one of my best clients. You're outgoing. You're persistent. You don't need me to hold your hand anymore."

This probably isn't true, but if it gets him out of his funk any quicker, there's no harm done.

"So . . ."

"So I want you to find that girl you have a crush on, go right up to her, and do your thing."

"Any girl?"

"Any girl. The world is your oyster," I say.

"I'm allergic to oysters."

I sigh. "How about carpe diem? Does carpe diem work for you?"

"It does. Thanks, Shane."

"No problem."

We both stand up and start heading back to the parking lot. I'm shivering.

"By the way," I add, "since when are you so emo?"

"What do you mean?"

"Why didn't we just meet at your house? You live like five blocks away from me."

Adam shrugs. "Good point."

13

"**FIRST OF ALL, YOU WOULD** not believe the amount of gunk that came out of my skin. I mean it was disgusting . . . *ly awesome.*"

"Come on, Reed. Gross."

It's gorgeous outside; the calendar may say February, but spring has already sprung in Kingsview. School ended a few hours ago, and I spent the afternoon running around like mad putting out a couple of client fires before meeting Reed here in the bleachers of the baseball field behind school to catch up.

A few players are stretching on the field, but it's an off day, so it's otherwise quiet. Reed and I are sitting on the third-base side. Behind us are the tennis courts, where Reed first attempted to hit a forehand volley into Marisol's heart. After several reschedulings and some uncertain moments, Reed finally had his first date with Marisol last night. I've been waiting all day for the download. I've folded an empty straw wrapper in my hands twenty times out of nervous anticipation.

"It wasn't gross," Reed continues. "It was strangely magical."

"You're sick."

Before I send my clients out on their first date, I make sure they take care of a few basic grooming needs. The predictable stuff is Q-tips in the ears and tweezing eyebrows, but I also had Reed buy Bioré pore strips. You put a strip on your wet nose, wait fifteen minutes for it to dry, and then rip it off. Out come all your blackheads. Sounds weird, but my clients soon swear by them. The only thing is, the very first time you use them and sixteen years of gunk comes out, it's not pretty.

"Reed, will you just get to the date?"

"You said you wanted details!"

"Not this much."

"Fine. So I picked her up. We went to the pizza place. We ordered some slices and sodas and stuff. *I* paid."

"Nice. Nice."

"She looked amazing. We talked about school for a little bit. And then . . ."

"And then *what*?"

"And then Rebecca joined us."

"What? What do you mean, Rebecca joined you?"

"I mean Rebecca Larabie was at the pizza place, too. She saw us, Marisol asked her to join us, and she did. I spent the rest of the night with the two of them, and they mostly talked to each other about student government. Except when Rebecca negotiated a discount on her meal with the owner because there wasn't enough pepperoni on her pizza. She really drove a hard bargain."

"Damn," I say. "They probably planned it."

"Planned what?"

"If a girl isn't totally sure she likes a guy yet, she'll sometimes have her friend 'randomly' show up on the date so that she's not stuck with him."

"Oh." Reed is crestfallen. "Noted." He scribbles forlornly in his notebook. Then he perks up. *"Or,"* he says, "maybe Marisol just wanted Rebecca to meet me. You know, feel me out a little bit because she's totally into me."

Reed looks at me expectantly.

"Or that," I say. "It could definitely be that." Who knows? Maybe it could. "I like where your head's at, Reed. You're staying positive. I'm proud of you."

"Thanks."

"But next time something like that happens, text me! Don't make me wait a whole day to find out! What happened at the end of the night?"

"Rebecca went home on her own, I dropped Marisol off, she pecked me on the cheek, and that was it."

"Wait, she kissed you on the cheek?"

"Yeah."

"Reed, way to bury the lead under a ton of blackheads. That's awesome!"

"Really? A cheek kiss is that big a deal? I dunno. I wasn't sure."

"First of all, an *unsolicited* cheek kiss. And second of all, a month ago you were wearing dumpy jeans your mom bought you, so let's keep things in perspective. I'm not a miracle worker."

Reed nods. "Fair enough."

I admire the cloudless sky for a moment.

Then all of a sudden I'm forced to scream: *"LOOK OUT!"*

Reed and I duck for our lives as a baseball flies over us, narrowly missing our heads and smashing violently into the bleachers about ten rows behind us with a *THWACK!*

At first I think it's a foul ball from batting practice. But then I spot Harrison marching toward the bleachers. I'm pretty sure he *threw* that ball.

"Uh oh," Reed murmurs.

Harrison's short fuse is well documented. His adrenaline is always pumping, and he never forgets a slight. That's probably what makes him a star athlete—and the last guy you'd want to have it out for you since seventh grade. He glares at us menacingly as he starts to climb the bleacher steps. His practice uniform has been hastily thrown on like he just learned of our presence and bolted from the locker room. In retrospect, the baseball field was probably a poor choice of locations for my powwow with Reed.

"I've been looking for you two," he says when he reaches us.

"Did you *throw* that at us?" I ask. "Are you crazy?"

"Calm down, Chambliss," he huffs. "I would have hit you if I wanted to."

"Congratulations," I say. "What's the problem?"

"You," Harrison says, pointing a finger in Reed's face. I have to admit, for a split second I'm actually kinda glad *I'm* not the problem for once.

"Me? What did I do?" Reed says.

"Were you out with Rebecca Larabie last night?"

"Uh . . . I mean, technically, but—"

"*I'm* with her."

It's a little scary how angry he is.

"I thought that was supposed to be a secret," I venture.

"And you!" Harrison repeats, now pointing his grubby finger at me. "Don't think I forgot about the college fair. What the hell were you doing with Rebecca? Were you hitting on her?"

"Oh, he was just running a wedge," Reed interjects.

"Shut up!" Harrison shouts.

Reed puts his hands up in surrender.

"If I see or hear of either of you talking to Rebecca again . . ." He cracks his knuckles. His message is loud and clear.

"All right," I say. "We're sorry."

Reed looks at me like I did something wrong. Hey, *sometimes* it's okay to apologize.

Harrison thankfully turns to leave . . . but then suddenly turns back and glares at me again.

"What now?" I say.

"Make sure you throw that in the trash."

"Huh?"

Then I realize he's referring to the straw wrapper in my hand.

"It's not cool to litter," he says.

Before I can even respond, he turns around again and exits down the bleachers.

Reed and I don't say anything for a full minute.

"What the hell just happened?" I finally mutter when we catch our breath.

"I have no idea," he says. "But you better throw that thing out."

14

TRISTEN HAS AN EXTREMELY busy social calendar, and it's been proving more difficult than I expected to lock down a night for our next date. So when she casually mentioned that she was going to the mall this afternoon, I offered to drive and take her to lunch. This is certainly not the romantic venue I envisioned for our second date and first solo affair, but I'll have to make the most of it.

First we check out the department stores, where Tristen has every cologne dealer douse me with a sample so that she can smell it. As per my advice to Reed, I like to spritz cologne into the air and then mosey through the cloud, but these salespeople are aggro and hitting me with direct shots. Once I get sprayed with the same cologne that Mr. K. bought, and I swear I almost puke. Still, it's a good time. And I must admit,

Tristen sniffing my wrists and my neck is kind of a turn-on.

After that, I tag along with Tristen to a few random stores. It's a fascinating experience. One moment she's asking a bewildered salesclerk if a piece of jewelry is made with conflict-free minerals, and the next moment she's using her iPhone to calculate what 10 percent off is. Did I mention she's wearing really short jean shorts? The front pockets are sticking out below the shorts and onto her thighs. Occasionally I forget my own name.

Next we walk to the food court for lunch, and I try to steer the conversation toward anything physical. If you're talking to a girl and the act of hooking up is mentioned, and she wrinkles her nose and says, "Gross," then you're probably never gonna hook up with her. But if she's comfortable talking about those things with you, then maybe, just maybe, one day she might be open to actually doing them with you. In the Galgorithm, this is known as laying groundwork for future physicality. It's one of my most advanced moves.

"What's that ChapStick you were using?" I ask.

"It's cherry," Tristen replies. "It's my favorite."

"But don't your lips taste like cherry after that?"

"Yes! That's the whole point. I can just smack my lips and it's like getting a little snack."

She smacks her lips. Oof. I'm sweating a bit.

"Which one do you use?" she asks.

"The blue one with the moisturizer."

"That's so boring!"

"How can my choice of ChapStick possibly be boring?"

"Like, let's say you kiss someone. Then they're just getting boring blue ChapStick flavor."

Aha! She brought up kissing!

"So what you're saying is, when *you* kiss someone, they get the cherry flavor."

"Exactly!" she says.

Now I'm gonna very subtly bring this around to me.

"Well, what if I don't like cherry?" I ask.

"*Everyone* likes cherry," she says with a smirk.

"Are you sure about that?"

"Pretty sure."

She smiles and touches my elbow.

For a second I think that this conversation has gone *too* well. We've stopped walking. Tristen is staring at me. I stare back at her. She smacks her lips again. Is this really about to happen?

"What do you want to eat?"

"Huh?"

"What do you want to eat?" she repeats.

She motions to all the restaurants in the food court, which we've just reached. Which is why we stopped. Which is why she's just standing there, waiting for me.

I snap out of it.

"Oh," I manage.

Shane, you think Tristen wants to kiss you next to a dirty KFC? Use your head. Your other head!

"I'm good to eat whatever you want," I say, recovering.

"Hey," Tristen says, "isn't that your friend Jak?"

I look up and see that Jak is indeed walking our way. I realize I never told her I was coming to the mall with Tristen. It was kinda last minute.

"Yeah," I say to Tristen, "it is."

When Jak gets closer, she notices me, then Tristen. Her face flashes briefly from surprise to confusion to *Oh, crap*. But it would be weird if she didn't say hello now. And I'm excited to see her anyway.

"Hey, buddy," Jak says as she reaches us. We exchange our typical high five.

"Hey," I say. "Do you know Tristen? Tristen, Jak. Jak, Tristen."

"We've seen each other in the halls," Jak says.

"Yeah. It's nice to, like, officially meet you, though," Tristen says. "Shane talks about you a lot."

"What? No I don't."

Jak smiles at my discomfort.

"Well you talk about her a *little*," Tristen says.

I shrug. That's fair. "What are you doing here?" I ask Jak.

"I had to get a present."

"Oh?" I say. "For *whom?*"

"Ah, nice call!" Jak says. "For my mom. Birthday coming

up. I was—" Jak stops to sniff the air. "What's that horrible smell?"

I look around. "I think that's me," I say. "We might have gone a little overboard on the cologne shopping."

Jak covers her nose. "It smells like sandalwood and sorrow."

I snicker. She always has a way with words.

"I think he smells nice," Tristen says.

Jak doesn't agree, but she lets it go.

"Jak," I say, "did you know that there actually *are* endangered dolphins in the Congo?"

"Yeah, right."

"It's true. Tristen was just telling me about it."

"Atlantic humpback dolphins," Tristen explains. "They live off the west coast of Congo and Gabon, but they're being hunted to extinction. I've been trying to raise money for an organization that supports them."

"You learn something new every day, I guess," Jak says.

"I like your sneakers, by the way," Tristen adds. "Are they vintage?"

We all look at Jak's beat-up white Chucks.

"No," Jak says, a bit offended. "Just dirty."

I grimace. Then I try to get this show on the road. "So, we were just gonna get some food . . ."

"You should join us!" Tristen says to Jak.

Jak looks at me and we communicate through best friend telepathy. She gets my message: *No.*

"That's okay, I already ate," she says.

"Are you sure?" I ask, although I'm just being polite.

"Yeah, I'm good. You guys have fun."

"Okay," Tristen says. "It was super to finally meet you."

"You too," Jak says. "Shane, text me later. Have a sweat-tastic day."

I grin. "Will do."

"Bye!" adds Tristen.

Jak exits.

That was a nice, albeit slightly awkward surprise.

Tristen turns to me. "What's a sweat-tastic day?"

"Just some stupid joke."

I appreciate the fact that Tristen doesn't ask for further explanation, and we continue to the food court. Stinking of sandalwood and sorrow, I begin to plan how to convert this second date into a third one.

15

TACO TUESDAY IN THE CHAMBLISS household is an intense experience. For much of the week everyone eats on a different schedule, but on Tuesdays my family has an unspoken agreement to be at the kitchen table by seven o'clock. Since I'm an only child, sometimes having this spotlight feels like being on stage, and other times it feels like being on trial.

I can already smell dinner when I get home at six forty-five. I've lived here since I was born, though the house seems to be in a constant state of remodeling. It's an open secret that my bedroom is next. I just know my parents are biding their time until my first day of college, when they can send me off into the world to become my own man and promptly turn my room into a walk-in shoe closet.

My dad has always done the bulk of the cooking, and

when I enter the kitchen, he is preparing ground beef on the stove with his shirt off. It gets hot in here, and he claims that cooking shirtless is the most efficient way to cool down. My dad is an engineer and makes even the most outlandish statements seem true and logical. People say we look alike and share the same hazel eyes, but I'm taller and can't match his grisly beard.

Fixins are my mom's responsibility. She's chopping onions and tomatoes, humming as she goes. She was a singer before becoming a music lawyer. Jak thinks her short blond hair makes her look like Ivan Drago's wife from *Rocky IV.*

"Meat's up!" Dad announces. He pours the ground beef into a bowl and my mom arranges the fixins as I complete my one and only duty, setting the circular kitchen table with plates, place mats, and utensils. We don't stand on ceremony after that: We all go to town and start making our own tacos.

"Dad, you think maybe you could put your shirt back on now?" I ask.

"Why? This is natural."

"Yeah, but one of your chest hairs is in the onions."

"Peter," Mom says.

Dad, on cue, reluctantly puts his shirt on.

"Shane, I've barely seen you the past few days," Mom says. "I need to hear some updates, please."

The last time I talked to my parents about girls in any real way was in the rubble of my breakup with Voldemort. They tried their best to console me. To be fair, Mom never really liked Voldemort. She caught one glimpse of the bar code tattoo on the back of her neck and decided she was no good for me. To be fair *again*, Voldemort usually kept it covered up pretty well, and I thought it was really hot. I guess the moral of the story is this: Listen to your mother, not a sixteen-year-old girl you met at a high school football game who has a tattoo she got illegally when she was underage.

I shrug and try to avoid my mom's request for news, but I know I won't be able to stall for long.

"I have an update," Dad chimes in. "I spent a hundred and twenty dollars on lottery tickets yesterday."

"No you didn't," Mom says.

"I did."

Mom doesn't look my dad in the eye, which is her way of telling him she's peeved. Dad's occasional reckless spending on lotto tickets and renovating the house is a sticky issue. I'm pretty sure my mom outearns my dad, which might chafe my dad, who fancies himself old school.

"What?" Dad says, in response to Mom's silent treatment. "It was Powerball. Three-hundred-million-dollar jackpot!"

"Well, did we win?" Mom asks.

"Yes, Kathryn, we won three hundred million dollars and I didn't tell you. I'd be halfway to Belize by now with my second family."

I laugh at this but Mom doesn't. She'll come around.

My parents met at a "cocktail party" in New York City in the early nineties. "Cocktail party" in quotation marks because I'm pretty sure it was a rave. One day I plan on getting the real story out of them.

"What about you, Shane?" Mom asks. "Anything to report?"

"Yeah," Dad adds. "Any gals at school we should know about?"

My dad, in his infinite wisdom, occasionally refers to women as "gals." I don't know if it's an old-school throwback or just something to tease my mom with, but it's become a running joke in the family. Which was why, when I needed a snappy name for a formula about girls, I knew right away what to call it: the *Gal*gorithm.

My parents, of course, have no idea that I moonlight as a dating coach. Keeping that secret requires a delicate balance of meeting my clients when my parents aren't around and taking advantage of their lenient curfew when I have to, say, run to the freakin' beach on a weeknight. But even outside of my consulting duties, when there's a gal, er, girl, I'm interested in—Tristen, presently—I no longer tell my parents about her. I'm too afraid that if I tell them about a girl I like, the next conversation we have will be me explaining to them that we broke up. It was hard enough with Voldemort—especially since she never gave me a reason—and I never want to go through that ordeal again.

"So?" Dad repeats. "Any gals? Anything?"

"Uh . . . ," I begin to stammer.

"Oh no!" Mom exclaims suddenly. "I forgot Yvonne's birthday yesterday!"

"No. That's your best friend," Dad says.

"Yes. I know. Oh my God, I have to call her right now. February twentieth!"

I feel bad she forgot Jak's mom's birthday. But I'll take anything to get out from under my parents' microscope for the night, even though I don't really mind all their questions. At least I know they care.

Strangely, it's moments like these that raise my anxiety level about graduation. Even though Taco Tuesday inevitably veers off into some kind of minor drama, at least it's consistent. It's my house. It's tacos. It's Tuesday. Once I go off to college, it's gonna be a free-for-all. Tacos any night of the week. But more importantly: life without the support system I've always had here in Kingsview.

16

I CONVINCED JAK TO PLAY hooky from English today so that we could go get lunch together on my free period. There's a bagel place as well as a Baja Fresh and a few other restaurants close enough to school to drive to. It didn't take much convincing to get Jak to cut. She claims that her proper usage of *whom* puts her in the 99th percentile of all English students nationally, and therefore learning any more would just be showing off.

It's still the transition period between classes, and I meet Jak at the front of the school, inside the main doors that lead to the courtyard. A surly-looking security guard in a yellow polo shirt keeps a watchful eye over the frenzy of students passing by.

"You're late," Jak says.

"Do I have time to go to the bathroom?"

Jak sighs dramatically.

"What?" I say. "I've had to go all morning. I'm dying here."

"Fine," she says.

I hurry to the nearby men's room. When I leave Jak, it strikes me that in all the conversations I've had with her recently, we've never once discussed running into each other at the mall when I was with Tristen. That's the kind of thing we'd usually break down frame by frame like the Zapruder film. I sort of got the impression that maybe Jak didn't like Tristen . . . but Jak never brought it up, so neither did I. Probably best to leave it alone.

When I return from the restroom, I notice that Jak isn't standing by herself anymore. She's talking to Adam. He's trying to explain something to her, and she's laughing. That in itself isn't weird. Adam and Jak know each other and have shared a handful of classes together over the years. But when I join them, Adam seems surprised—and perhaps disappointed—to see me.

"Oh, uh, hey, Shane," he says.

"What's up, Adam? How are ya?"

"Not much," he replies.

What a doofus.

"Listen to what just happened," Jak says to me. "Adam asked me to borrow a pen for class, but he already *had* a pen behind his ear." She shakes her head in amusement.

That's odd, I think.

Adam turns slightly red and holds up the pen in question. "I'm an idiot."

"Yeah you are," Jak says.

"It's the glasses," Adam says. "Sometimes I forget I have things behind my ear."

"That's what she said," Jak adds.

Adam forces a laugh, but I don't even think it's one of Jak's better jokes.

"Right," I say. "Adam, so you're all sorted with pens? 'Cause we're gonna grab some lunch. Let's talk later."

Jak and I turn to leave, but suddenly Adam spouts, "I like your sneakers!"

We pause and instinctively look at our feet. I'm wearing flip-flops. So he must be talking to Jak, who's wearing her usual grimy Chucks.

"Um, thanks," Jak says, genuinely appreciative.

"I like Converse, too," Adam says. "What do you think about their new line?"

"They're cool. And everyone says I should get a new pair," Jak says. "Or at least wash these. But that seems like a lot of effort."

"I agree," Adam says. "You shouldn't do either of those things."

Wait a minute.

I suddenly realize what's happening. *Adam is hitting on Jak.* That's why he's all awkward and nervous. That's why he's laughing at Jak's dumb jokes. Jak must be the girl Adam told me he had a crush on at the beach! The one I encouraged him to go after!

The pen trick was an icebreaker I mentioned to Adam when he was pursuing Olivia and was afraid to talk to her: Go up to a girl with a pen behind your ear and ask her to borrow one. She'll notice you already have one and call you out on in it. Next thing you know, you're in a conversation. Not only that, but . . . complimenting her on something unusual, demonstrating common interests, asking open-ended questions, agreeing with whatever she says . . . these are all tips I've imparted to Adam before.

He's using the Galgorithm on Jak.

Adam definitely knows that Jak is my best friend. So why wouldn't he just tell me that he was interested in her? I mean, I guess I *did* insist he didn't need me anymore and that he'd be better served by going it alone. But still. That must be why he was so thrown when he saw me come back from the bathroom.

Between mentioning getting set up and coveting a textual relationship, Jak *has*, in her own special way, been insinuating that she's looking for a boyfriend. Jak likes tall guys, and Adam is towering over her right now as they continue their inane conversation, which has branched out from sneakers and into shoelaces. Adam is smart enough to be able to understand most of Jak's obscure references and picky enough to appreciate Jak's aversions to, well, just about everything.

Adam and Jak . . . it could happen.

That said, it doesn't have to happen right now. And I'm hungry.

"Guys," I interject. "Are we gonna . . ." I motion to Jak and the exit.

"Oh, right. Lunch," Jak says.

"Cool. No problem," Adam says. "Sorry about the pen thing. I've been a little all over the place since things ended between me and Olivia." He lowers his chin toward his chest for effect, a shameless play of the pity card.

"I heard you guys broke up," Jak says. "That sucks." This may be the most empathy I've ever seen her display.

"Thanks. It's been tough," Adam says. "But I'm doing my best to get over it." He glances at me briefly and then turns back to Jak. "We should hang out sometime."

"Sure," Jak says.

Adam says nothing. It feels like he had scripted the entire conversation up to this point and is now drawing a blank.

Jak is forced to chime in. "Maybe one day after school. Wednesday?"

"Ooh, I have anime club on Wednesdays." Adam says.

Now it's Jak who doesn't respond. So awkward. I feel like I'm on shore, waving bon voyage to the *Titanic*.

Adam at least attempts to continue the conversation. "Have you heard of anime club?" he asks.

"I know you have to be a virgin to join," she replies.

Ooh, jab right to the gut.

I'm taking great pleasure in this, and I don't quite know why.

"I'm just joshin'," Jak adds quickly.

"You know what?" Adam says. "Screw it. Wednesday would be perfect."

Skipping anime club is as carpe diem as Adam gets.

"Cool," Jak says.

"I have all your contact info," Adam says. "From that project we did in earth science freshman year."

A little weird, but okay.

"I'll, uh, text you or whatever," he continues.

Jak nods.

Adam looks at Jak and then he looks at me, not quite sure what to do next.

"I gotta get to class," he says finally, before turning and hurrying way.

Jak and I look at each other, both a bit bewildered. I raise my hand in the air.

"Up top," I say.

She smiles and high-fives me, and then we head out the door to lunch.

I try to push any uneasiness I have about this development deep, deep down, as far as it will go.

17

BEHIND THE MYSTERIOUS DOOR that leads to the teachers' lounge I always imagine the faculty in their underwear, drinking beer and smoking cigars. The reality is much more mundane. The room is about twice the size of a normal classroom and has a few couches, coffee tables, desks, and a semi-enclosed kitchenette area. Everyone is fully clothed, sober, and smoke-free.

I'm dropping off a thank-you note for one of my teachers who wrote me a college recommendation, but she's not here, so I put it in her mailbox. I'm about to leave when I hear a voice I was truly hoping not to hear.

"Shane!"

It's Mr. Kimbrough, who emerges from the kitchenette area with a cup of coffee and waves at me. Although I told him during our last conversation that I would try to think of a way for him to secure a real date with Ms. Solomon, I've actually been trying to avoid him. Between my own love life and my actual clients' love lives, I've got a lot on my plate.

Mr. K. beckons me to join him at one of the desks in the lounge. I sigh and then head over to him. He greets me with what I find to be an overly enthusiastic handshake. "Good to see you, Shane!" Well, at least he doesn't hug me.

"What's going on, Mr. K.?" I ask. "Sorry I haven't been in touch."

"I figured you were cooking up some really good advice for me."

"Something like that."

"Anyway, I'm glad you're here. I'm been trying to get my mind off . . ." He looks around warily at the handful of other teachers in the room. None are within earshot. "*Deb*. You know, so I don't obsess and what have you."

This is him *not* obsessing?

"I started a blog," he says. "I want you to check it out."

Eleven words that no one ever wants to hear.

"A blog?" I say.

"Yeah." He opens an old IBM laptop. "I'm gonna post interesting math stories. Maybe a few jokes and cartoons." He launches the site and then steps back for me to see. "I call it Humble Pi."

The blog features a caricature of Mr. Kimbrough, which,

given the generous hairline and stingy waistline, he probably drew himself. Under the title BOB KIMBROUGH'S HUMBLE π is another drawing, this one of a literal pie—like the dessert—with a pi symbol bursting out of it.

"Humble Pi. Get it? 'Pi' as in 3.14?"

"I get it," I say.

"It was either that or Divide and Conquer."

"Stick with Humble Pi."

"Okay. Good idea."

"You haven't posted anything yet," I mention.

"I just started it. It's only for me and a few of my math-teacher friends. I doubt anyone else will even care."

Now that's the understatement of the century.

Mr. K. is admiring this WordPress site like it's his first-born. I'm not really sure what he wants from me right now.

"So . . . I'm gonna take off," I say.

"Crap!" Mr. Kimbrough exclaims suddenly. He slams the laptop shut, almost clipping my fingers.

"What?" I say.

Mr. K. motions with his chin: Across the room, Ms. Solomon has entered the lounge and is walking toward us.

I continue to be impressed by Mr. K.'s taste. Ms. Solomon has stunning green eyes and long, Rapunzel-worthy dirty-blond hair. She's slender and wears a white blouse tucked into a black pencil skirt—teacher-appropriate but sexy enough to inspire, I'm sure, a few naughty daydreams from her male students. She smiles as she approaches us.

For some reason, Mr. Kimbrough panics and tries to hide his laptop under a stack of papers.

"Hey, Bob," Ms. Solomon says as she reaches the desk. "I forgot my lesson plan."

She plucks it right from the top of the stack on the laptop, without ever noticing or caring what's underneath.

"Hey, Deb," Bob says.

Ms. Solomon smiles again and then turns to leave. Mr. K. speaks up.

"Deb, do you know Shane? He was one of my best students."

She pauses and turns back. "No, I don't believe we've met."

"Hi," I say. Finally I am formally introduced to the mythical Deb! "My best friend is actually in your class. Jak."

"Jack?"

"Jennifer Kalkland."

"Oh, right, of course. She's wonderful. Very quiet."

I chuckle at the thought of Jak ever being quiet. "That's only when there's a roomful of people," I say. "Around me I can't get her to *stop* talking. And it's usually nonsense."

"Lines on curves, huh?" Mr. K. interjects.

"Lines on curves?" I say.

"Tangents. Your friend goes off on tangents."

I look at Mr. Kimbrough. Now is not the time for esoteric geometry humor.

"Tangents," Deb says. "I get it. Very clever."

She grins. Bob blushes, but seems to loosen up.

"Come on, Shane, *I* taught you geometry. And I just told Deb you were one of my best students!"

"That's okay," Deb says. "We can give Shane a free pass on that one."

Alas, like Adam with Jak, Mr. Kimbrough doesn't seem to have a follow-up to keep the repartee going. Conversing with girls is not easy!

But I notice the way Deb looks at Bob. She didn't cringe at his terrible joke. In fact, she seemed to genuinely enjoy it. She clearly has to get back to class yet is still lingering. She just used the word "we." Obviously she was joking, but subconscious actions explain a great deal.

Damn it, Shane, I think. I'm such a sucker for a long-shot love story. And observing Mr. Kimbrough and Ms. Solomon right now . . . well, I think they've got a chance. Despite Mr. K. being a little needy and all my instincts telling me not to get involved, I know I have to help him. What kind of dating coach leaves a man behind? I gotta come up with a plan on the spot.

"Mr. Kimbrough," I say, improvising, "I meant to thank you for that restaurant recommendation. My parents went to Laredo Grill and they loved it."

Mr. Kimbrough looks at me quizzically. "What?"

"You know . . . ," I say, trying to relay as much subtext as humanly possible. "Laredo Grill, that Mexican place you recommended I tell my parents about. *Remember?*"

This conversation never happened, of course. I saw Laredo Grill on a banner ad on Yelp the other day. But I think Mr. Kimbrough is starting to catch my drift.

"Oh. Right. Yeah . . ."

"Supposedly they have great margaritas," I say. I glance at Ms. Solomon. She arches her eyebrows ever so slightly. I have no idea what that means.

"And also awesome fresh guacamole," I add.

"I love fresh guacamole!" Ms. Solomon exclaims.

I don't know much about women in their twenties, but from what I've seen on TV they usually like margaritas and/ or guacamole.

There's another lull in the conversation. I feel like I am boring holes in Mr. Kimbrough's head as I try to convey to him what to say next. Unfortunately, we don't have best friend telepathy like me and Jak.

Mr. K. gasps slightly—the lightbulb goes on; I think he's got it! He turns to Deb.

"If you like guacamole, maybe the two of *us* could go to Laredo Grill together and eat some. You know, at night. My treat."

Ms. Solomon looks at me and then back at Mr. Kimbrough. "Like a date?"

Mr. Kimbrough glances at me. I try to imperceptibly but still perceptibly nod my head *yes*.

"Sure," Mr. Kimbrough says, thankfully taking my cue. "Like a date."

Ms. Solomon smiles. "That would be great. I'd love to."

Booyah!

Now Mr. Kimbrough is just standing there with a perma-grin on his face. Ms. Solomon checks her watch.

"Oh no!" she says. "I totally lost track of time. I'm late for class. I'll talk to you later, Bob." She smiles at him. "Nice to meet you, Shane."

"You too."

She hurries off. When she closes the door of the teachers' lounge behind her, Mr. Kimbrough has still not stopped smiling.

"It's okay, Bob. She's gone. You did good."

Mr. Kimbrough suddenly embraces me in a great big bear hug. I'm about an inch off the floor. I go stiff as a board. He finally puts me down. The other teachers are oblivious.

"Shane, thank you! You are the best wingman ever."

"Don't worry about it."

"Does this mean you'll keep helping me?"

I take a deep breath.

"Yeah, I'll help. As long as you—"

Before I can finish, he embraces me again.

This time I roll with it.

18

WHEN WE FIRST GOT to the theater, and the movie we wanted to see was sold out, I thought this date with Tristen was gonna be a bust. Then she suggested we go back to her house and watch TV, and I tried to play it cool but also couldn't drive fast enough. Her parents are out for the night, and her younger sister is at a friend's house. The only problem is, Tristen hasn't given me any indication as to when any of them will be home, so there's both excitement and terror in the air.

There are clothes and books and shoes and makeup scattered all over the floor in Tristen's bedroom. You can barely see any carpet. She has a MacBook in a pink case with a Greenpeace sticker on it. We sit on the edge of her bed both because it's in front of the TV and also because there is literally no place else to sit. Tristen sits to my left and loads the On Demand menu to look for something for us to watch.

"What are you in the mood for?" I ask.

"Something funny," she says. "Maybe something with Will Ferrell. *Or*, there's this documentary about fracking I've been dying to see."

These are confusing times. Tristen and I have really hit it off. She's sweet and kooky and opinionated. It's been a while since I allowed myself to *like* like anyone. This could be the real deal. But even though Jak and I have never explicitly discussed it, it does still kind of bother me that Jak doesn't like Tristen. Again, that's not based on any empirical data, just more of a hunch. I know I shouldn't care, but she's my best friend and I can't help it.

Tristen scrolls through the movies on-screen. She's wearing ripped, super-faded jeans. Considering her usual wardrobe, the top she has on is fairly conservative, meaning it's sleeveless and pretty sheer.

If I were advising one of my clients in this situation, I would tell him to be patient. When a girl wants you to make a move, she'll give you the signal.

"So," Tristen says, "when was the last time you were in a relationship?"

I'm caught off guard.

"What do you mean?" I ask.

"What do you mean, what do I mean?" she says. "Like when was the last time you had a girlfriend?"

Wow, Tristen does not mince words. I respect that.

"It's been a while," I admit. "A few years."

"Really?"

"Yeah. I mean, I've 'seen' girls here and there. But nothing serious."

"Why not?"

Yeah, Shane, why not?

"I don't know," I say. "I guess I haven't found the right person."

"So you're picky?"

"I wouldn't say that. Maybe I just know what I like?"

I say it like a question because I have no idea if it's true or not.

"Have you ever had your heart broken?"

"Boy, I'm really getting interrogated tonight."

"I'm sorry," she says. "You don't have to answer that."

I think she's definitely flirting with me and will eventually want me to make a move. Yet we've never even hooked up and it seems like she's already sizing up my boyfriend potential. I don't want to look a gift horse in the mouth . . . but I also don't want to put the cart before the horse. Basically any proverbs with horses are trouble.

I decide to answer her honestly. "Yes. I have had my heart broken. Once. It was really bad."

"What happened?"

"I don't really know . . ."

This is partially true. In some respects, I know exactly why Voldemort broke up with me. I lacked the maturity and confidence that girls expect, and I ran afoul of most of the flirting, grooming, and dating faux pas I now counsel my clients to avoid. But even though I'm aware of these things in my brain, in my heart I still want answers. One day Voldemort wanted me, and the next day she didn't. What changed?

"Are you okay?" Tristen asks.

"Huh?"

"You just trailed off and got really quiet."

"Oh. Yeah. Sorry."

"It's okay. But I gotta say—the girl who broke your heart, whoever she is, didn't deserve you."

Tristen is not shy. And she's into me!

"Thanks," I say. "I've been having a really good time hanging out with you."

"Me too. I guess we have Anthony and Brooke to thank for that."

"You mean Hedgehog and Balloon?"

She laughs. "Exactly."

"By the way, why is Brooke's nickname Balloon? Hedgehog I get."

"Actually, I have no idea," she says. "Maybe it's better as a mystery."

Yeah, I say to myself, *unlike when your parents are coming home.*

Tristen reaches the end of the list of On Demand movies.

"Well, that's all of them," she says. "Nothing I really want to watch."

"Me neither."

She smiles and looks me in the eyes, then looks at my lips for a split second, then back to my eyes. *That's the signal!*

I put my left hand on her back, between her shoulder blades. Testing the waters. She doesn't flinch. I can feel her bra clasp beneath her shirt.

I lean to my left and move my face toward hers.

She closes her eyes . . . and we kiss!

Her lips are soft and interlock naturally with mine. I reach over and caress her face—her skin is really smooth, and I can feel her two little moles. She darts her tongue tentatively into my mouth and I respond in kind. The sloppiness factor is low; we have good kissing chemistry right off the bat.

The world around us starts to get blurry. The specter of her family coming home, the books and clothing getting trampled beneath our feet, the stress and doubt I feel every day . . . gone.

I trace a line with my hand down her cheek and to her neck. She presses her tongue deeper into my mouth and tenderly bites my lower lip. This has already been the best date ever, and the night could end right now and I would be thrilled, but I'm feeling bold, so I move my hand from her neck to her chest.

She moans softly and wraps her arms around me.

We continue kissing.

Cherry ChapStick never tasted so good.

19

I WANDER INTO PERKIN'S BEANERY, where Tristen and I had our first date, and am immediately surprised to see Adam sitting at a table by himself. He's cleaning his glasses when I walk up to him.

"Yo, man."

"Hey, Shane." He looks at me, puzzled, and shakes my hand.

I notice he doesn't have any coffee. "What are you doing here?" I ask.

"I'm actually meeting Jak," he says.

"You're kidding."

"No. I texted her to see if she wanted to get together. I offered to pick her up, but she said just to meet her here at four."

"Well that's weird," I say.

"Why?"

"Because Jak asked me to meet her here too."

"Huh? She double-booked us by accident?"

Wait. It's all starting to come together.

"Ah. No. I don't think it was an accident," I say. "She told me to meet at 4:15. I'm just really early. I think she wanted me to show up and check in with her depending on how your date was going."

This is exactly what Marisol and Rebecca did to Reed.

"So, like, as an excuse in case she wanted to bail?" Adam says.

"Nah. More like just a friendly face in case she panics. I wouldn't worry too much. You'll be fine."

"Ah. Okay. Thanks. So . . . I guess you might as well sit down, then."

"Yeah, sure. I can't wait to see the look on Jak's face."

I take the seat across from Adam. He's arranging and rearranging the napkin dispenser and container of stirrers on the table. Clearly nervous.

I look around to make sure that Jak hasn't arrived yet. "So I have to ask," I say. "Why didn't you tell me that Jak was the girl you had a crush on?"

Adam grimaces. "I'm sorry. I feel really bad about that. Are you pissed?"

"No, I'm not pissed at all." At least I don't think I am.

"It's just that," he continues, "you made that whole speech about how I should just do it on my own and I didn't need you anymore."

"Totally. I get it. But Jak *is* my best friend. I might have been able to help."

"I know. But I was afraid that if I started talking about it, I would lose my nerve. You know how I am. I think too much and freak out."

"Oh, I know."

"I feel bad. Are you sure you're not mad?"

"I'm sure. I'm just surprised it's Jak."

"You told me I needed to move on. And I've always kind of had a thing for her."

"Okay. Well, listen, just treat her right."

"Absolutely. Of course. Thanks for being so cool about it."

Adam wipes a nonexistent smudge from the face of his watch and rearranges the napkin dispenser once more.

Maybe I am a little peeved that Adam didn't tell me about Jak. I mean, in a way I'm proud that he was able to approach her like that in school without my help. But a little heads-up would have been nice. Then again, now that Tristen and I are an item—not boyfriend and girlfriend, but definitely an item—maybe I should start taking my nose out of other people's business and focus on my own.

"She's coming!" Adam says in a loud whisper.

We observe Jak entering the coffee shop, absentmindedly

playing with her Fitbit. Her hair is out of control. I feel like it's close to brushing against the door frame as she passes. She's wearing a thrift store Led Zeppelin T-shirt. I guarantee you she has no idea what Led Zeppelin is.

She notices me and Adam sitting together and does a similar double take to the one she did when she ran into me and Tristen at the mall: *what?* followed by *uh oh* followed by *the hell with it.*

Adam starts to fidget even more as Jak approaches.

"Don't worry," I say. "I won't stay long."

We both stand up.

"Shane," Jak says, trying to act surprised. "What are you doing here?" She is a terrible liar.

"Really?" I say. "That's the route you decided to take? Pretending not to know I was coming?"

"I don't know. I was making it up as I went along. You're early."

I shrug. We high-five.

She turns to Adam. "Hey."

"Hey," he says.

"So, yeah," Jak says, "I kinda invited Shane, too, but I thought he was gonna come later, and, I don't know. I'm not good at this stuff."

"Don't worry about it at all," Adam says. "We just had a chance to catch up."

"Yeah, I'm gonna take off in a minute," I say. Just long

enough to make sure Jak is okay. And I figure it doesn't hurt to see if they have any chemistry.

"Can I get you something?" Adam asks Jak.

"Thanks. Yeah. I just need to think about what I want for a second."

Adam pulls out a chair for Jak and the three of us sit down.

It's quiet and a little awkward. I lob anything out there to break the silence.

"Jak, are our moms still fighting?"

I keep Adam in the loop: "Our moms are best friends. My mom forgot her mom's birthday. It's a whole thing."

"I think they made up," Jak says.

"Good," I say.

"Are you close with your mom?" Adam asks Jak.

"Pretty close. She's a little crazy."

I eye Jak.

"I know," she says instantly. "I'm a little crazy too."

"Hey, I didn't say a word," I add.

Adam emits one of those fake giggles you do when you're feeling left out of the conversation. I don't really want to go, but I realize I'm stepping all over his game. When Jak and I are together, we tend to drown everybody else out.

"Okay," I say, standing up. "You guys enjoy."

I sense a flicker of disappointment in Jak's eyes.

"Take it easy, Shane," Adam says. He shakes my hand.

"Later, hater," Jak says.

I leave as she and Adam begin consulting the chalkboard menu.

Jak smiles like a goofball.

Adam, I can't help thinking, is a lucky guy.

20

I'M SITTING WITH REED at one of the cement tables in the courtyard in front of school. He's hit a bit of a rough patch in his quest for Marisol. Like Mr. Kimbrough, Reed made the mistake of not confirming a second date at the end of the first one. I blame myself for not hammering that into his head. But I thought he could recover and Marisol would be receptive to a return engagement. Instead she has been stonewalling him.

I've decided to shake things up a bit. Unbeknownst to Reed, Tristen is meeting me here in a few minutes to say hello. She's bringing along Marisol; they both run in the junior-class popular crowd. I'm hoping that getting Reed and Marisol talking face-to-face will jump-start things between them. It's too easy for her to blow him off via

Facebook or text. In person that bag of bones can be rather charming.

Right now, though, Reed is pretty down in the dumps. I take my clients' successes and failures personally—probably to an unhealthy degree—so I'm just as bummed as he is. But it's my job to rise above and steer the ship.

Reed is glumly looking through his little notebook for answers, but I tell him, "You're not gonna find what you're looking for in there."

"Maybe Marisol isn't interested anymore," Reed says. "Maybe that kiss on the cheek meant goodbye. Maybe she's too good for me."

"Reed, Marisol puts her pants on one leg at a time, just like you. Stay positive. You're doing great."

"If you say so."

"Listen, here's what I want you to do the next time you see Marisol: *Be yourself.* Forget everything I've told you. Forget the Galgorithm. Forget your notebook."

"But I never got *any* girls being myself."

"That's ridiculous. I know you pretty well by now, Reed. And you're awesome. If you saw in yourself what I see in you, you'd be singing a whole different tune right now."

"Really?"

"Really," I say.

Usually I tell my clients to try to *remember* everything I've taught them, not to forget it. But Reed is getting too bogged down. He needs to learn to think on his feet. Heck, in four months I'm graduating and he's gonna have to fend for himself anyway.

"By the way, I have some news for you," I add.

"What?"

"I'm kinda sorta seeing Tristen Kellog."

Reed's eyes light up.

"Tristen? Like"—he makes the international symbol for big boobs with his hands—"Tristen?"

"Yup."

"You, sir," Reed continues, "are a god among men."

One fringe benefit of seeing Tristen is that it gives me even more credibility with all my clients. Not that Reed hadn't already drunk the Kool-Aid.

"How did *that* happen?" he asks.

"I'll tell you about it later. Oh, and another thing: Tristen is on her way right now, and she's bringing Marisol."

"What?"

Tristen and Marisol are indeed approaching us from the other side of the courtyard.

"Is this an ambush?" he says.

I feel bad, but I know that putting Reed on the spot is the right move. He needs to be taken out of his comfort zone.

"Reed, don't panic. Just be yourself. This may be your last chance, so *do what your heart tells you to do.* Okay?"

"My heart is telling me to puke."

"Don't do that."

"It's also telling me to run."

"Go with whatever your third instinct is."

Reed gulps. He hides his notebook, and we stand up as Tristen and Marisol arrive. I notice that Tristen and I are not on lip-kiss-hello terms yet. Marisol and Reed share a slightly awkward but still warm greeting.

"Tristen," I say, "have you met Reed?"

"No, I don't think I have. Nice to meet you, Reed."

Wow, there are still girls in Reed's own class who actually don't know he exists. It's almost impressive. It also makes me wonder if Marisol has ever even mentioned him to Tristen before.

"Nice to meet you, too," Reed says to Tristen. "Marisol, you look pretty today. I like your shirt."

"Oh, thanks." Marisol is not much of a blusher, but I definitely think I see a touch of red. Reed is not holding anything back. By the way, Marisol is wearing a plain white T-shirt, so that compliment came out of nowhere. I'll take it.

"What are you guys doing?" Tristen asks.

"Just hanging out," I say.

"I was actually helping Shane with his Euro homework," Reed interjects.

"What?" I legitimately have no idea what he's talking about.

"You know, since you're failing history, I need to tutor you."

"You're failing history, Shane?" Tristen asks.

"No. We're not even in the same class."

"That's how bad it is," Reed says. "He didn't know how long the Hundred Years' War was."

This catches Marisol off guard. She giggles and almost spits out her gum.

And now I realize what's happening. Reed is turning the tables on me for his own benefit. Poking fun at me to make himself look good.

"Right, Shane?"

"Right," I mutter. Now who's getting ambushed?

"He once told me it's really freezing in Moscow, and that's why they call it the Cold War."

Marisol laughs again at my expense.

I must admit, Reed can be quite clever. And I'm happy to be the fall guy. But he's testing my limits.

"I mean, Tristen," Reed continues, "what do you see in him? He thought World War One was started by Franz Ferdinand. The band."

Now Tristen and Marisol are both laughing *with* Reed and *at* me. I think that's enough.

I grab Tristen's arm. "Why don't we, uh, get outta here or take a walk or something?"

"All right," she says. Then, turning to Marisol, she adds, "He's funny." She's talking about Reed.

Pickup artists much more professional than me call this

"social proof." It's basically when a girl gets approval about a guy from the people around her. Marisol just witnessed Reed getting social proof from Tristen, the prettiest girl in school. That's no small accomplishment.

Tristen and I say our goodbyes. Tristen and Marisol still have the giggles, and I can't get out of there fast enough. I nod to Reed as we exit, as in: *I did my part; now it's time for you to do yours.*

As me and Tristen are walking away, Tristen says to me, "Oh, that's *Reed*. You know what, Marisol said she had gone out with a guy, but I didn't realize that was him."

So Marisol *did* mention Reed after all. Even better.

Tristen reaches out to hold my hand. In the moment, I almost don't fully appreciate it.

"You know he was kidding about me failing history," I say.

She doesn't seem to care either way.

When I casually glance back to see how Reed is getting along with Marisol by himself, I am absolutely astounded. They've been on their own for thirty seconds. We're on school grounds. It's the middle of the afternoon. And it's now clear to me what Reed's third instinct was, after puking and running.

Reed and Marisol are making out!

21

JAK WOKE UP THIS MORNING to find two more complimentary passes to Sweat Republic in her e-mail. I figure it was
either a display of persistent marketing or a misguided apology for our odd encounter with Sarah with an *h*. Regardless,
Jak decided it was a sign that we should continue our workout
kick. So we geared up in headbands and Under Armour, drove
to the gym, walked the floor several times to determine just
how we were gonna kick off this most sweat-tastic of days, and
then beelined to the smoothie bar, having completed exactly
zero exercise. My Fitbit just reads YOU DISGUST ME.

We ordered our smoothies from a bewildering menu
inside and are now drinking them outside, sitting in silver
metal chairs under an umbrella on the sidewalk. From here
we can observe our fellow Sweat Republicans—as I'm sure

they're not called—enter and exit the gym (sorry, *more* than just a gym).

This QT is long overdue for several reasons. The rest of Jak and Adam's coffee date went well, and they went out again. I'm happy for Jak but slightly concerned that things between us have been a little . . . let's just say "off" lately. Certainly the presence of Tristen and Adam in our lives has begun to put a crunch on our already dwindling time together. But it's more than that. Crushes have come and gone in the past, and it's never before affected me and Jak's status as partners-in-crime. I can't quite put my finger on what's wrong, but I'm glad we have this chance to catch up.

"What did you end up getting?" Jak asks me.

"Black pepper mango pumpkin."

She looks at my smoothie. "Why is it brown?"

"I don't know," I say. "I thought it would be orange."

"How does it taste?"

"Honestly, it's the best thing I've ever had in my entire life."

Jak smiles.

"What's yours?" I ask.

"Jicama honey basil."

"Gross. And?"

"I don't even know what jicama is, but this is so good I want an IV directly in my bloodstream."

"Basically, they should close the gym part and just open up a chain of smoothie bars."

"I would invest," Jak says.

She sucks down half her smoothie in one go. She's still wearing her headband, and it's nice to see her without all that hair in her face for the first time in, well, probably years.

"So," Jak says, "let's get down to business. I need all the dirt on Tristen. Tell. Me. Everything."

"Things are going well. You know, we haven't had a conversation or anything about it, but I'd say we're seeing each other."

"Oh I figured *that.*"

"Well, that's really everything."

Jak doesn't say a word.

"You want to know about her boobs, don't you?"

She shrugs.

"I told you I don't boob-touch and tell."

"Aha! So you *have* touched them!"

"That's not fair. You tricked me. Fine, yes, I've touched them."

"Well?"

"Tristen is a very interesting, well-rounded person . . . who just also happens to have very well-rounded boobs."

"Ha! I need to tweet: 'Shane Remains the Mane! #tristenaccomplished.'"

"Don't tweet that."

"What, you don't want the world to know you're dating the hottest girl in Kingsview?"

"She's also a good person."

Jak bursts out laughing. My face doesn't change.

"Oh," Jak says. "You weren't kidding."

"No, I wasn't kidding. You think I'm that superficial?"

"Um, yeah."

"Well I'm not. Tristen is cool."

"This is the same Tristen Kellog who writes about jeggings in the *Chronicle*?"

"Yes. Why? Do you not like her?"

The million-dollar question.

"I like her," Jak insists. "But you promise you're not just dating her because her body is both a temple and a wonderland? It's like a temple *in* Wonderland."

"I promise."

I guess I feel a little better having asked Jak flat-out about Tristen, although I still don't totally believe her. It's strange; it's not like Jak to be territorial. No one wants me to get over Voldemort more than she does. Maybe I'm looking too far into it.

"I'm just watching out for you, Chambliss," she says. "You're a boy, so you have a brain the size of a pea."

"Yeah, maybe like a really big pea."

"Good one," she says sarcastically. And then she polishes off her smoothie.

"What about you?" I ask. "What's going on with Adam? Spill it."

"You know, we're hanging out. He seems all right."

"Come on, Jak, don't get shy on me now. Details."

"Well," she says, "he complains a lot, which I can appreciate. He's really tall, which I like. I mean, he wears these stupid-looking glasses that someone must have told him looked good."

Ouch. "I think they're hip," I offer.

"Nothing is hip if you have to say, 'I think they're hip.'"

Fair enough.

"But besides that, I dig him," she says.

"I'm surprised, Jak. Usually you can come up with more flaws than just a pair of glasses."

"What can I say? I'm getting soft in my old age."

"Have you . . . hooked up?"

I'm surprised by how nervous I am to hear the answer to this question.

"Maybe we kissed or whatever."

Hmm. There you have it. Reed is kissing Marisol. Adam is kissing Jak. I'm so proud of my clients. Well, more so Reed. I'm not sure how I feel about Jak and Adam yet. He's right for her, but is he, like, perfect for her? I don't know.

"You promise you're not hanging out with Adam just because you're—"

I catch myself.

Jak is quick to pounce.

"What were you about to say? Lonely? Desperate?"

"No, no, no. Not at all."

"Wait, are you *jealous*?"

"No!" I insist.

"Because you're the one who told me that guys talk about me with their penises out in the locker room."

I laugh, and this breaks the tension.

"I know," I say. "I didn't mean anything like that. I was just being dumb."

I finish my smoothie.

"I miss this," Jak says. "You. Us. Sitting around talking about nothing. The last few months you've been like totally distracted. We need to do this more."

"I agree."

She reaches across the table and takes my hand. It's an odd gesture, but it's also really nice. We look at each other and smile—a smile only two best friends can share.

"It feels so good," Jak says wistfully, "to be holding the hand that touched Tristen's boobs."

I grab my hand back. "Come on, Jak."

She cackles.

"I'm sorry, Chambliss, but—"

"I know, I know. It was a perfect moment and you had to ruin it."

I shake my head. Jak is just so darn pleased with herself right now.

"Hey, remember we were joking about going to one of

these house parties before the school year is up?" I ask.

"Yeah," she says, "to drink a lot and make poor decisions. I remember."

"There's gonna be a big kegger next week. We should go. If you're feeling up to it."

"So a house full of alcohol and people being friendly?"

"Yup, that's basically the definition of a party."

"Shane, I know you usually don't go to these things because—"

"You get anxious and freak out."

"Exactly. And that's pretty cool of you to have my back. But for you, I think I can handle one party. I'm game if you're game."

"I'm game if *you're* game."

"Then it's settled," Jak says. "We're in. I'm kinda excited. Is someone gonna spike the punch? Does everyone put their keys in a fishbowl and go home with a stranger?"

"If you're going to a party in an eighties movie, then yes."

"What? I don't know."

"It's probably just gonna be a lot of standing around," I say.

Jak smiles at me.

"Now *that* I can handle."

22

IT TOOK A LOT OF PLEADING and a little subterfuge, but I managed to convince my parents to move this week's Taco Tuesday from our house to Laredo Grill. They're under the impression that I merely wanted to change things up a bit and check out a new restaurant, but of course I have ulterior motives. Mr. Kimbrough and Ms. Solomon are having a date here tonight, and I promised Mr. K. that I would be on hand should he need me. I told him that I would help him with Deb, but I have not copped to my other consulting duties and clients, nor have I mentioned the Galgorithm. He just thinks I'm good at giving friendly advice, and I plan on keeping it that way.

There's no shortage of Mexican food in Kingsview, and it seems Laredo Grill has chosen to differentiate itself by offering unnecessarily trendy spins on typical dishes and charging an arm and leg for them. I guess there's demand out there for thirty-dollar grilled sea bass tacos, because the place is packed. While my parents are out of earshot, I talk to the hostess and request a specific table I see available. I want to be close enough to observe Bob and Deb, who are already seated, but far enough away that I won't be made.

I rejoin my parents in the waiting area, but soon get a nice surprise: Hedgehog and Balloon have just finished dinner and are walking our way.

"Shane! Hey!" Anthony says.

The three of us exchange hugs and greetings. Anthony's little spikes have been gelled flat—the executive Hedgehog look.

"I want you to meet my parents. Mom, Dad, this is Anthony and Brooke, my friends from school."

They all shake hands. "It's lovely to meet you," Mom says.

"Have you eaten here before?" Brooke asks.

"First time," Dad says.

"You're gonna love it," Anthony says.

"Is it a special occasion?" Mom asks.

Hedgehog and Balloon gaze at each other lovingly.

"It's our eight-and-a-half-month anniversary," they say simultaneously.

"Aw, jinx," Brooke says, and kisses Anthony on the nose.

Mom thinks this is utterly adorable. My dad is too hungry to care.

"I'm so sorry, Mr. and Mrs. Chambliss," Anthony says, "but my dad is waiting to pick us up outside."

"No problem. It was great meeting you. Have a good night," Mom says.

"You too," Brooke says.

I take a moment to recognize that I'm standing with two of the most amazing couples I know. For all the hoops I jump through—and instruct my clients to jump through—that's all anyone's really looking for: a partner who gets you, who loves you unconditionally, and who's always there to listen.

"Aren't they cute?" Mom says to my dad.

"Blue-cheese enchiladas," he replies. He's now reading the menu and not paying attention.

Hedgehog and Balloon exit and the hostess arrives to take us to our seats—but not the seats I requested. Our table is much farther from Bob and Deb than I would have liked, but before we sit down, I notice Deb get up and walk away. She's wearing a flowery dress and heels; she came to play.

"I'm gonna use the bathroom," I say to my parents. "I'll be right back."

"Have you thought about what you want to order?" Mom asks.

"Mom, it's Taco Tuesday. I want tacos." I turn to my dad. "Wait, you're not gonna take your shirt off, are you?"

Dad shrugs, as if you never know.

I leave our table, take the long way around the restaurant,

and get to Bob. He's wearing a button-down shirt and navy blazer, and is pulling it off nicely. I'm grateful I won't have to take him to the mall for an episode of *Extreme Makeover: Slovenly Man Edition*. I double-check that my parents can't see me from here.

"Shane, you made it!" Mr. K. says.

"I told you I would. How's it going?"

"So far, so good." He dabs beads of sweat from his forehead with a cloth napkin. "Deb went to the restroom."

"Listen," I say, "I can't really see you well from where I'm sitting, so you're pretty much on your own unless there's an emergency. Do you have it under control?"

"Yes. I think so. I mean, I could use all the help I can get."

What works on a high school girl might not work on a more sophisticated woman like Ms. Solomon, so I've been doing some research.

"When Deb gets back," I say, "look her in the eyes and ask her if she uses Latisse."

"Latisse? I don't know what that is."

"But women do. It's prescription eyelash lengthener. By asking her if she uses it, you're indirectly complimenting her on having nice long eyelashes."

"Shane, you're a genius."

"Nah, just a kid trying to help you out."

I manage to jet from Bob's table just before Deb gets back from the bathroom and blows my cover. I take the long way around the other way and end up back at my parents' table.

"Did I miss anything?" I say.

"Your father just ordered a very expensive cocktail," Mom says.

"Kathryn, enough. We're having a nice dinner. When in Rome."

"I don't think they had eighteen-dollar mojitos in Rome."

Dad considers this. "Then why don't you split it with me?"

"Sure. But it better be the best nine bucks I ever drink."

It's always unsettling when my parents squabble in front of me, even if it's good-natured.

My mom turns to me. "You really couldn't comb your hair? You look like you're in an out-of-work boy band."

"Mom . . ."

"Well, coming here was your idea," she continues. "So are we celebrating something? How was your day? How was your week? Your mother needs some news about her favorite and, coincidentally, only son."

Crap. I've drawn too much attention to myself by insisting we take Taco Tuesday out on the road. I'm about to get grilled like the sea bass. I definitely don't want to talk about Tristen.

"Uh, actually, I was wondering if you guys could tell me the story of how you met."

My parents look at each other.

"We met at a cocktail party," Dad says. "You know that."

"Come on," I say. "You were at the same college at the same time and you're saying you didn't meet until after you graduated?"

My parents look at each other again. They have their own brand of telepathy, and my mom silently gives my dad permission to tell the real story.

"Okay, fine," Dad says. "Freshman year of college your mom was in an a cappella group. She had—and still has—a very beautiful voice. I was in the AV club. A real nerd, unlike the super-cool guy you see before you today. They were recording a CD, and I was the sound engineer. Me and your mom just hit it off."

"What's a CD?" I deadpan.

"Ha ha," Mom says. "Just you wait. One day you'll be old too."

"So you met recording an album? That's the whole story?"

"Well that's how we *met*," Dad continues. "After that we were just friends. Then we became best friends. And it wasn't until five years later, after college, that we finally got together as a couple."

"At the cocktail party in New York," I say.

"Well," Mom admits, "actually it was a rave."

I knew it!

"But we were already best friends," she says. "That's just when we first . . . as you would say, hooked up."

"Gross, Mom."

"It's what happened."

"I don't understand. Why not tell people you met in college?"

"Every married couple has a real backstory, which is usually pretty boring, and then the embellished version, which they tell everyone," Mom says. "Back then we thought it was more romantic, you know, that we saw each other across the room at a party and fell in love. At least more romantic than meeting in a dingy sound booth in the basement of our dorm and then only getting together five years later. It was pretty anticlimactic in real life."

"And once you tell so many people the embellished version, you start to forget what really happened," Dad adds. "But the fact is, I married my best friend."

He puts his arm around Mom and kisses her. After all these years, my parents are still looking at each other as affectionately as Hedgehog and Balloon do now.

"Even though it all worked out for us, there's a very valuable lesson I want you to take away from this story, Shane," Mom says.

"What's that?" I ask.

I think I already know the answer. It's a tale about friendship, love, patience, and fate.

"Don't go to raves," Mom says. "They're very dangerous, and who knows what they put in those drinks."

Or that.

23

IT'S A COOL, STARLESS FRIDAY night. A little chilly for March, but pleasant nonetheless. One of the seniors on the baseball team is throwing a bash in his backyard. His yard is about half as big as mine, and is hemmed in by a wooden fence, so it seems pretty packed and loud for a gathering of fifty people. There are two kegs, a few tiki torches, a Jambox playing Top 40, and plenty of red Solo cups and ice. Meaning that in the scheme of parties I've been to, this is a real classy affair.

I found out about the party through Tristen, who's typically in the know about everything. She has a birthday party to attend first and is meeting me here in a bit. I dragged Jak here after she agreed to go and then tried backing out. She insisted on having two rum and Cokes at her house first to "calm her nerves," and then we walked over together. Jak told Adam about the party, and he came separately. This is probably his first jock party but, hey, act like you belong somewhere and they'll let you in. Rebecca is also here, shaking hands and kissing proverbial babies even as her presidential term begins to wind down. I'm sure Harrison invited her, though their status remains unclear. Harrison himself is lurking about somewhere, but I decided that if Jak can overcome her fears to show her face here, so can I.

Currently Jak is holed up in the corner by one of the kegs, drinking another beer and making me keep her company. I pour myself one, too.

"Guess what," she says.

"What?"

"Today Ms. Solomon said we're not gonna have any more pop quizzes for the rest of the year."

"Really? Nice."

"She was in a weird mood." Jak leans in close to my ear. "I think she got laid. . . ."

I silently pray that Jak is right and Mr. Kimbrough is responsible.

Jak nods her head, as if confirming her own hunch. "Her hair looked different. I can tell."

Her breath reeks of booze.

"Maybe you should slow down on the drinking a bit, champ," I suggest.

"Maybe you should slow down your face."

"That doesn't make any sense."

Jak's social anxiety has always straddled the line between clinical and her just being a weirdo. She does not like people, present company proudly excluded. Still, one on one, two on one, or even three on one she can manage, make conversation, and generally observe basic societal customs. But in any group larger than that, she can't deal. She copes with it through denial, only hanging out with me, and, tonight, Malibu and Diet. Over the years I've gone to a few parties without Jak, but usually I bend over backward to keep our plans just the two of us. Tonight will be an interesting test.

Jak gives me the stink-eye for commenting on her drinking. Then she spots Adam approaching and starts fixing her hair, an impossible task that I rarely ever see her attempt.

"Hey, guys!" Adam says as he reaches us.

"Yo," I say, and we shake hands.

"Hi, Adam," Jak says, in a voice one octave higher than usual.

"Hey, Jak." He gives her a kiss on the cheek. "You smell nice."

"Thanks."

I know for a fact that she smells like cheap rum and Coke.

"Are you guys having a good time?" Adam asks.

Ten times out of ten, Jak will answer that question with, "Meh."

"Yeah," Jak says, "it's a great party."

For some reason this response bothers me. I mean,

whatever. It's an okay party. And we're stuck in the corner. Adam smiles at Jak. She manages a smile in return and then downs the rest of her beer.

The three of us are soon joined by Rebecca. She has a sweater tied around her neck, which isn't a thing I thought people actually did. We exchange pleasantries. Jak ekes out a hello.

"So what's going on over here in the corner?" Rebecca asks.

"Whole lotta nothing," Adam replies. He and Rebecca clink their keg cups. They run in the same overachiever circles.

"Shane," Rebecca says, "I meant to tell you—we finally sorted out that senior parking permit issue."

This was the conversation I had with her at the college fair, in order to wedge her away from Marisol, and then totally forgot about.

"Oh," I say. "Great."

"Let me ask you guys something," Rebecca continues. "What would you think about a *second* extracurricular period after school? That way students who are in multiple clubs can juggle two meetings in one day."

Jak deadpans: "There's a *first* extracurricular period?"

Even in her hour of weakness, Jak still knows how to land a joke.

Adam, however, lights up at Rebecca's suggestion. "That

would be amazing. I've been requesting that for years. Right, Jak? Wasn't I just telling you how busy I am?"

Jak is pouring another beer from the keg. "Sure. Okay."

Adam turns to Rebecca. "What can we do to make this happen, and quickly? I would love to help." The hardest-working nerd in Kingsview apparently wants to squeeze even more in before graduation.

"That's great," Rebecca says with a winning smile. "I'll message you next week to discuss. Here's my card just in case."

"Excellent," Adam says, taking the card, admiring it, and smiling back.

Jak shifts on her feet. We are at her maximum occupancy for civil behavior, and seeing Rebecca chat up her crush isn't helping. I feel uncomfortable altogether, so I try to lighten the mood by innocently putting my hand on Rebecca's shoulder. "Who would have thought we'd be making school policy at a keg party, huh?" I joke.

Of course, as soon as I do this, Harrison enters our little corner, carrying one black garbage bag and one green garbage bag. "Listen up—"

He stops midsentence when he notices that I have my hand on Rebecca's shoulder. That's the only tell I need to know they are still hooking up. I immediately remove my hand.

"What I was about to say was," he continues, "trash goes in the black bags. Cans and plastic cups go in the green bags."

Adam, who I sense may be emboldened by half a beer, chimes in: "I never pegged you for an environmentalist, Harrison."

Harrison zeroes in on Adam. "I'm sorry. *Who* are you?"

Adam blanches. "Uh, Adam Foster. We've known each other since elementary school."

"I'm kidding, dummy. I know who you are."

This draws an uneasy laugh from the rest of us.

Harrison starts to crack his knuckles.

Jak looks worried, but also a little glassy-eyed.

"Is there something wrong with caring for the environment?" Harrison asks Adam.

"Harrison," Rebecca says, trying to calm him.

Adam wisely says nothing.

"My moms are activists," Harrison says. "Do you have a problem with my moms being activists?"

Adam vehemently shakes his head no.

"I didn't think so."

Everyone in our circle is silent. But then the standoff is interrupted by Jak, of all people. She finishes her beer and throws her plastic cup in the green bag that Harrison is holding.

"Thank you," Harrison says, quite graciously.

"You're welcome," Jak says. And then she lets out a small belch. She already has a fresh cup at the ready.

The tension seems to be defused. Adam breathes a sigh of relief. Harrison grows bored with us and turns to leave, almost running smack-dab into Tristen, who has just entered the party, nearly spilling her beer.

"Excuse me," Harrison says.

"Sorry!" Tristen says.

Then Harrison does a double take: He looks at her body and then back at her face. I've seen that reaction around Tristen a thousand times. Her cleavage is total kryptonite.

"Oh, hey, Tristen," he says.

"Hi, Harrison."

I don't even want to know how they know each other.

Harrison exits. A moment later Rebecca pretends to see a friend and shadily sneaks away, though I know she's headed after him.

Tristen and I kiss hello—on the lips. That cherry ChapStick gets me every time.

"I'm glad you made it," I say.

"Me too," she says. Then: "Hi, Jak!" She hugs Jak, who is clearly not expecting it. Then she turns to Adam: "Have we met? I'm Tristen." Before Adam can even reply, she turns back to me: "Did I miss anything?"

"Not really," I say.

I realize it's just me and Tristen and Jak and Adam left in the corner. You would be hard-pressed to find two more unlikely pairs.

Tristen holds my hand. Jak notices this. She holds Adam's hand. Adam is clearly surprised by—and amenable to—this development. We stand in silence for a minute, drinking our beers with our free hands.

Tristen suddenly remembers something, gives me her beer to hold, digs into her purse, and pulls out a small bottle of vodka. "I almost forgot—I brought this as a gift."

"That was nice," I say.

"My mom taught me never to go anywhere empty-handed," Tristen says.

"Now I feel bad that I didn't bring anything."

"We can say it's from both of us. My mom also taught me to share."

"Your mom is very generous."

"Yeah. Total Sagittarius."

I don't know what that means. "Um, okay."

Tristen looks at the bottle of vodka in her hand. "The question is," she says, "who do we give it to?"

"*Whom*," me and Jak say simultaneously.

"Huh?" Tristen says.

"It's whom. *Whom* do we give it to," I say. "Not who."

Jak smiles.

Tristen looks at me blankly, and then at Jak with just a hint of derision.

"You guys are being weird," she says.

Tension has returned to our little circle. Jak lets go of Adam's hand. She's sweating a bit. After a few moments, she excuses herself. "I gotta get some air."

"Should I come with you?" Adam asks. "Also, we're already outside."

"No. Thanks." Jak leaves and disappears into the party.

"Now, *that* was weird," Adam says.

"Nah. That was just Jak," I say.

"You really do talk about Jak a lot," Tristen says.

"I don't know. She's my friend." I look at Adam. I feel bad for him. I feel bad for Tristen. I'm acting weird. I'm having crazy thoughts. I'm a little tipsy.

"I need to go to the bathroom," I say.

I leave Tristen and Adam standing there and bolt.

I navigate my way through the party and into the house through a back door—no easy task, as the backyard has swelled with even more people. The house itself is pretty big and a lot ritzier than mine. It takes me a few minutes of searching before I find the guest bathroom upstairs. I just want to throw some cold water on my face. But I try the door and it's locked. I lean against the wall in the hallway, trying to wrap my head around everything that's happening.

I hear an argument coming from the guest bedroom next to the bathroom. The door is slightly ajar. My curiosity gets the best of me, so I peer inside. It's Harrison and Rebecca. They're sitting on the bed, fighting.

"I don't understand why we still have to be a secret," Rebecca says. "Are you embarrassed by me?"

"Of course not," Harrison says. "You're amazing. It's just . . . my parents."

"Why do you care so much about what they think?"

"You know why."

"I'm sick of sneaking around!"

"Rebecca, please—"

Uh oh. Harrison spots me spying on them through the crack in the door. I've been made. "What the . . . ," he says.

Harrison stands up and starts making his way toward me while Rebecca shouts at him. I close the door. In a panic, I try the guest bathroom again. This time it's open.

I lunge into the bathroom, slam the door behind me, and lock it, temporarily at least barring Harrison from killing me.

Then I hear groaning.

I'm not alone in the bathroom.

Jak is on her knees in front of the toilet, vomiting.

"Shane is the Mane," she manages, pumping her fist meekly.

24

AFTER WAITING A FEW MINUTES to make sure that Harrison has either lost interest or been waylaid by Rebecca and is no longer lurking behind the bathroom door, I manage to scrape Jak off the floor. I put her arm around my neck and very carefully help her stumble out of the bathroom, down the stairs, and out the front door of the house, away from the party and without anyone noticing. At this point she is mumbling incoherently. I've never seen her like this.

Jak's house is closer than mine and her parents are out of town, so I decide that's our best bet. I put my arm around her waist and hold her as tightly as I can. She can't walk on her own, or in a straight line, and she stops to puke every block or so. It should take ten minutes to get to her house. Instead it takes almost thirty. It barely registers that we left Tristen and Adam just standing there at the party.

It's a tricky maneuver, but I open Jak's gate with one hand while keeping her steady with the other. We head to the front door. Jak didn't bring a purse, so I have to stick my hand into the front pocket of her skinny jeans and fish around for her keys.

"Buy me dinner first," she mutters.

Luckily, her house is all one level. I help her in the front door and down the main hallway to the bathroom that's adjacent to her bedroom. I flip on the lights and Jak shields her eyes like a vampire. Her bathroom is fairly small, with just a one-person sink attached to the wall below the medicine cabinet, a shower in a claw-foot tub with the curtain already pulled aside, and a toilet squeezed into the little space in between. She's such a low-maintenance girl that I'm surprised by how many bottles of hair stuff and skin stuff and other goo are scattered everywhere. It's like a TSA evidence locker in here.

Jak is covered in puke and in general is a mess. I pull her Chucks off her feet and then help her into the tub, standing up and otherwise fully clothed. I take her phone out of her pocket and her Fitbit off her wrist and put them on the sink. Then I stand off to the side, outside the tub, but always keeping a hand on her to prevent her from tipping over, and turn the shower on. She spits and claws at the water like a baby bear cub getting a bath. The front side of her shirt and jeans sorta gets cleaned off, but I realize that washing her clothes is futile.

I turn the shower stream away from her and toward the wall and start to strip her down. I help her pull her shirt over her head. We spend a solid ten minutes trying to get her jeans off because they were skintight to begin with and are now soaking wet, but somehow we manage. Now she's only wearing a bra and underwear. I notice she has not even made an attempt to match them.

"Everything is gonna be okay," I say.

I've seen Jak in a bikini a million times before, so this isn't that big a deal. Yet something is different. Even as recently as last summer she was gangly: all knees and elbows. But since then she's rapidly grown into herself. She looks fantastic—for someone who is simultaneously shivering and dry-heaving—and it feels weird to be seeing her like this.

I turn the showerhead back on her, and raise it up so that I can try to clean her hair. But Jak is too wobbly, and it's getting difficult to keep her standing, plus my hand is getting stuck in her hair, so now that most of the mess is cleaned up, I let her sit down in the tub. I turn off the shower and start to run a bath.

In a few months we're gonna be a thousand miles apart and I'll no longer be able to take care of her like this. She won't be able to take care of me. For the most part we've avoided discussing how we feel about the whole thing. It's been one big denial party. Right now goodbye doesn't even seem like an option.

Jak is starting to say something, but it's hard to hear her.

"Grin two," she mumbles.

"What's that?" I say.

"Grintoo."

"Jak, I can't understand you."

She musters the strength to speak clearly.

"Get. In. Too."

"Jak, come on. I'm already soaked."

She reaches up and tugs at my arm. It's clear she won't be listening to reason or taking no for an answer.

I sigh. "Okay. Hold on a second."

I start stripping off my clothes, which are wet and covered in Jak's vomit.

"Wooo, take it off," she murmurs.

I remove my Fitbit and place it next to hers on the sink. I get down to my boxers and shut off the water. Then I step into the tub and sit behind Jak, so that she's in my lap. Jak pulls her knees into her chest. I hug her tightly. A half-naked white guy and a half-naked black girl embracing in a bathtub. We look like a Benetton ad.

It occurs to me that this is the very same spot where our parents took that picture of us in the bathtub almost eighteen years ago. It triggers a flood of happy memories. What are the odds that our friendship would have lasted this long?

It's really quiet in the bathroom. I soothe Jak. Rub her shoulders. Tell her she's doing great. Occasionally she dry-heaves. But the worst is over.

When I'm with Jak I've found that I never want to be anywhere else. Whether it's in the bathtub right now picking puke from her hair, or lying next to her in a hammock staring up at the stars. Sure, I've pointed to her social anxiety as the reason I rarely go to parties or hang out with anyone but her. But maybe it's simply because I don't *want* to hang out with anyone but her.

"Jak," I whisper into her ear, "why did you drink so much?" As if there is ever a logical answer to that question.

I feel her shoulders shrug ever so slightly. "Adam. Tristen. Dunno," she whimpers.

My mind begins to race. Why did I really wait to tell Jak that Hedgehog and Balloon wanted to set me up with Tristen? Why was I so excited to see Jak at the mall on my date with Tristen? Why do I care what Jak thinks about Tristen? And most importantly, why does it bother me to see Jak with Adam? When Jak accused me at the smoothie bar of being jealous . . . was she right?

I squeeze Jak even tighter. I can feel every breath she takes. Every cough rattles her rib cage. I'm confused. I'm not thinking straight. Maybe my parents' story has gone to my head.

But then I think about me and Jak. Our telepathy. Her

way with words. How she finds the flaws in every single person on earth. Everyone except for me.

This low rumble in my heart. This fog that's been clouding my brain.

Oh my God.

I have feelings for Jak.

She stirs in the water. For a second I think I might have said that out loud. But I haven't, and she settles down.

I can't have feelings for Jak, I tell myself. I'm just getting nostalgic. I'm scared about graduating and leaving home. We're a platonic superduo and always will be. She's my best friend.

But she's also beautiful. And brilliant. And hilarious.

None of it matters anyway, because it will never be. In the wake of Voldemort, Jak told me explicitly that this was a line she would not cross. We will never be more than friends. She's been consistent about that point ever since.

Except when she randomly holds my hand or tells me she misses me or gets jealous when I'm dating someone else . . .

My mind is racing. I press my lips into the back of Jak's hair, near her neck.

I don't want to feel this way. I don't want to risk our friendship. I don't know what I want.

Jak yawns.

Very slowly, I start to turn her around in the tub so that she's sitting facing me. Her bra is soaked through to her breasts. Her hair is matted down on her forehead. Her eyes are half closed, and a single droplet of water rolls down the tip of her nose. But she still manages a grin.

Jak always says that perfect moments make her feel uncomfortable, and that's why she has to ruin them. But I know it's just a defense mechanism. Nothing could ruin this moment.

I caress Jak's face with my hand.

She looks up expectantly.

I search for the right words to say.

Jak opens her mouth, as if she's about to interrupt me and tell me exactly what I'm feeling.

I hang on her next breath.

And then she vomits right into the tub.

25

I CAN TELL MY CLIENTS the optimal time to ask a girl out. I can help them interpret her body language. I can determine whether text, Facebook, or Instagram is the proper channel for flirtation. But there are some scenarios for which my skills are woefully inadequate.

For instance, let's just say you think you might have romantic feelings for your best friend but you're not really sure and you don't really know *what* you're feeling and then when you're about to say something to her, she vomits. How long should you wait before trying to bring it up again? Three days? A week? A lifetime? There are no right answers.

Jak remembers little from that night. She knows she got smashed at the party. She knows I helped her get home in one piece. Besides that, she hasn't asked, and I haven't offered any more details. Things between us are fine. Stable to perhaps a bit awkward, but that will pass. If anything, she's embarrassed by the whole thing. And this from a girl who does not easily feel shame. She once told me that she only has four feelings: happy, sad, bored, and umami. She is such an endearing weirdo.

Meanwhile, I'm left to wrestle with my own, much more complicated feelings. I thought that maybe I just had a moment of weakness in the bathtub. Maybe I was just a little buzzed. But when I woke up the next morning, my feelings for Jak, whatever they are, were still there. I don't really know what they mean and I don't even know if they're real. I would certainly not be the first guy to confuse jealousy and nostalgia for actual affection. Never mind the fact that I'm dating Tristen, and Jak long ago declared herself off-limits anyway. The whole thing is confusing and compounded by the dangerous level of hormones flooding my soon-to-be-eighteen-year-old body.

While I continue soul-searching, I've decided there is one person I can open up to about my conflicted feelings for Jak: Adam. And, yes, I realize he seems like the last person on earth I should be confiding in. But he and Jak have been hanging out for a few weeks, and I feel like I should be honest with him, guy to guy. He's a client and a friend, and I don't want to keep him in the dark. Maybe since he knows both me and Jak he can even shed some light on the whole situation, or at least tell me I'm being crazy. At the minimum, Adam owes me enough to listen to what I have to say. And that's why I've come here, to anime club.

I open a door in the administration hallway to find an all-purpose classroom with a television and a DVD player at the front. I go unnoticed by the ten or so hoodie-clad male students who are watching a trippy Japanese cartoon. I cannot follow a second of it. More importantly, Adam is nowhere to be found.

"It's called *Fullmetal Alchemist*."

I jump when I hear Adam behind me.

"What?" I say as I turn around.

"*Fullmetal Alchemist*," Adam says. "That's what they're watching. One of the most popular anime series of all time."

"Got it. Why aren't you in there?"

"I was with Rebecca. She was upset."

I was the only person who witnessed Harrison and Rebecca fighting at the party, and one of the few who even knew they were going out in the first place. But since then I've heard through the grapevine that they split up.

"Is she okay?" I ask.

"Yeah, she's fine now. She wouldn't actually tell me what was wrong. We've been working on her proposal for a second extracurricular period."

"How's that going?"

"Pretty well. Rebecca is something. There's a surprising amount of legwork that needs to be done in order to get it approved, and she just powers through it."

"I heard she once negotiated down the price of her pizza because there wasn't enough pepperoni on it."

"Um. Okay. I mean it wouldn't surprise me."

"Just think," I say, "two extracurricular periods after school means double the anime."

"Right. So . . . did you just come here to hang out or what?"

"Well, there's kinda something I wanted to talk to you about."

"Actually, me too," he says. "What happened at the party? You just left. And so did Jak. I can't get a straight answer out of her. Did you guys go home together?"

"Yes and no," I say.

"Um . . ."

"I mean, I took her home, but I didn't, like, 'take her home.' She just got too drunk and needed my help. It was a best friend thing."

"Why didn't she just tell me that?"

"Why does Jak do anything she does?"

"True."

"But the thing is, when I was helping her, I started to think . . ."

Adam looks at me.

"Think what?"

"I started to think that maybe I have feelings for her."

"Oh," he says. *"Oh."*

"It's probably nothing. I'm probably just confused. But

it's been weirding me out. And I wanted to be totally honest with you."

He takes a deep breath. "Well, I appreciate you saying something."

"I know I'm putting you in an awkward position."

"I'm not sure what you want me to do."

"Tell me I'm crazy."

He considers this. "Jak is awesome. So I get where you're coming from."

"So I could *not* be crazy?"

"Shane, you're the relationship expert. Why are you asking me?"

"Good point."

"Do you want me to back off?" Adam says. "Is that what you're saying?"

I begin to regret bringing it up at all. Because the truth is, I don't know *what* I want.

"No," I say. "I mean, you do whatever you think is right. I just wanted to be totally honest with you."

"You said that already."

"Oh."

"I feel like I should back off," he says. "You know what you're doing. I mean, it was you who said I should go after Olivia when no one else on the planet believed it was possible."

"Yeah, but Olivia cheated on you and left you crying at the beach like a Taylor Swift video."

"Ouch."

Sometimes I have to remind myself how much sway I have over Adam. He really looks up to me. I shouldn't abuse that.

"I think this might have been a mistake," I say. "Forget I even said anything."

"It's kind of a hard thing to forget."

"I know, but just try. It's been a weird few weeks. Don't listen to me."

"All right . . . ," he says.

I look into the classroom. "Get back in there," I say. "Enjoy your cartoon."

Adam furrows his brow and reluctantly joins his anime club comrades.

I'm left standing in the hallway alone. I don't feel any better. I'm not thinking any clearer.

I hear cheers and claps coming from the classroom. I wish I could join them in their fantasyland. Because my reality is more confusing than ever.

26

IF THE GALGORITHM HAS a birthplace, it may very well be Crescent Park. It was here that Voldemort broke up with me, sending me into a tailspin.

The park is in the center of town, about ten minutes from my house. It's nothing special. Just a basketball court, a little playground, and a couple of benches. What I like about it— check that, what I *used* to like about it—is that since the park is nestled in a residential area, it never really gets completely dark. It's surrounded by nearby porch lights and streetlamps, so even at night you can still see about twenty feet in any direction. It's like permanent dusk.

Voldemort and I used to come here, sit on a blanket, talk, and make out. I was in awe of her. Older, wiser, a bit of a baby face but with perfect dimples, soft hands, and that red hair.

She used to wear these flannel shirts I could never unbutton. She would do it for me and then we would roll around on the blanket together. I wished we could roll around on that blanket forever. Until she told me that she wanted to see other people. And that those other people did not include me.

The light plays tricks on you in this park. Tonight I'm here sitting on a blanket with Tristen, but every once in a while a shadow will fall on her face and I have to remind myself she's not Voldemort.

Me and Tristen planned this outing well before the keg party. It was her idea to have a picnic, and she had never heard of Crescent Park, but I suggested it. I figured it had been more than three years since I'd been here. Those demons must have been exorcised by now, right?

"I know I've been a little cagey since the party," I say.

"'Cagey'? Is that the politically correct term for shady? Every time I bring it up, you change the subject," Tristen says.

"I know."

"You left with Jak, didn't you?"

"Yeah," I say. "But it wasn't what you think. She was throwing up."

"Oh no! Poor thing."

"It happens."

"So that's it?"

Well, that and the fact that I've been examining every moment of the past seventeen and a half years of my life to try to figure out what my true feelings for Jak really are.

"Yeah, that's it."

"I think it's sweet," Tristen says.

"You do?"

"Yeah. You took care of your best friend. You're loyal. That's one of the things I like the most about you. Most guys are jerks."

She kisses me on the lips and lingers there for maximum effect.

My brain is scrambled. Like lightning hit a satellite dish and ruined the reception in my head.

"So you're not mad?"

"No, I'm not mad," she says. "I mean, I wish you would have just told me the truth. After you left, I talked to that kid Adam for a while. He's really weird. He said that the beer was too cold. How can beer be too cold?"

The strange thing is, the more Tristen reveals herself as patient and kind and just totally chill, the more conflicted about her I become. Not to sound like Adam here, but can a relationship be going *too well?* Tristen is amazing. And she's a knockout. Everything is great. But the thought that this is too good to be true keeps gnawing at me.

She runs her hands through my uncombed hair. "Where are you?" she asks.

"I just have a lot on my mind," I reply.

Jak, namely.

Tristen starts to kiss my neck. I tense up and pull back ever so slightly.

She looks at me. "Are you upset that I didn't know how to use 'whom'?"

"What?"

"'Whom.' That little inside joke you and Jak have. I was curious, so I looked up the proper usage. Turns out 'whom' is dying out, Shane. Some people don't even use it anymore. So you can't hold that against me."

"You looked it up."

"Yeah," she says. "I'm working on a new piece for the *Chronicle* and I thought I might be able to use it."

"I really appreciate the fact that you looked it up. But no, I'm not upset."

She starts to kiss my cheek and then my ear.

The last time I was in this park, I had my heart broken. I've had my guard up ever since. But what if, in the course of protecting myself, in the course of finding other people *their* soul mates, I miss the real thing?

"Shane," she whispers in my ear. "Relax. This is right."

She grabs my face with both of her hands and kisses my lips again. Then her tongue is in my mouth, against my tongue. I half go with it, half remain tense.

"Tristen . . . ," I manage.

She kisses my neck again and then goes back to my ear.

She nibbles on my earlobe. That gets me every time. I almost wish my attraction to Tristen were merely physical. But it's not. I genuinely like her. *Which is a good thing,* I tell myself.

If Voldemort hadn't broken up with me, I never would have created the Galgorithm, which means I never would have befriended Hedgehog, which means he never would have gone out with Balloon, which means they never would have set me up with Tristen, which means I never would have ended up back in this park tonight. So maybe this is fate. Or maybe I need to get out of my head and *just go with it.*

I put my hand on Tristen's cheek and kiss her. I press her onto the blanket. Only the blanket has gotten bunched up and we're just kissing on the ground. I don't care. She doesn't either.

The grass feels nice underneath our bodies, and Tristen feels right in my arms.

27

I CUT CHEMISTRY IN ORDER to hang with Jak during her lunch period. The early April sun is high in the sky, and this is the first really hot day of the year. Instead of driving to lunch, we've opted to be lazy and lounge under the shade of the cafeteria awning. It seems like Jak has cobbled together a meal from things she found in the backseat of her car: carrots, Doritos, and a giant gobstopper.

We've texted a bunch since the party but haven't spent a lot of time together, nor have we discussed what exactly transpired.

"So," Jak says, "I basically vommed on you. That happened."

She's cutting right to the chase.

"You remember that?"

"I don't remember much, but I do remember that."

"Although I would love to make fun of you for the rest of your life for puking in your own bathtub, it kind of makes me nauseous just thinking about it. And I'm not even eating. So why don't we agree to never speak about that part again."

"Chambliss, you have yourself a deal."

She starts to gnaw on the gobstopper. Personally, I would have gone with the carrots first.

"The thing is, before the, uh, reverse-peristalsis incident," she says, "you touched my face."

"Uh . . ."

"We were looking at each other in the tub and you kinda stroked my cheek like a creeper."

"Boy, you say you don't remember much, but you seem to remember a lot," I say.

"Solid deflection."

Typical Jak, never letting me get away with anything.

"I wasn't 'stroking' your cheek, I was just making sure you were okay," I say.

"By stroking my cheek?"

"I wasn't—I was just—I was worried about you. I wanted to make sure you didn't pass out."

"Hmm. Okay." She relents, thankfully. "Well, either way, I guess I should say thank you."

"For what?" I ask.

"You're gonna make me say it, aren't you?"

"Yup."

"Fine. Shane Xavier Chambliss, thank you for rescuing me from that bathroom, for carrying me home, and for taking care of me. I don't know what I would do without you."

"You're welcome. But you know my middle name is Aaron, not Xavier."

"Yeah, I know, but your initials are *SAC*. And you can't be Sac if I'm Jak. That's too many *ack*s."

"So my new middle name is Xavier?"

"Correct. I would *also* like to take a moment to thank God that you don't know how to take off a bra; otherwise I basically would have been naked in that tub."

"Jak, you are really bad at getting blackout drunk. You remember everything."

"It's a gift."

"And I know how to take off a bra."

"Do you, though?"

"You want me to take off your bra right now?"

"Go easy, Chambliss. I'm just giving you a hard time."

"I know."

"You're a good friend," Jak says. "The best."

And maybe that's all I'll ever be. And maybe I'm fine with that.

"Can I ask you something, Shane?"

"Sure."

"Did I do anything else dumb at the party that I *don't* remember?"

"I think at one point you had your flip-flops on the wrong feet."

"I do that all the time." She picks up her feet from under the table. "They're on the wrong feet right now."

They are indeed. What a nut.

"That's the only thing I can think of. Why?" I ask.

"Well, not to be a lame-o or anything, but Adam has been acting kinda weird."

Uh oh.

"Like what?" I ask.

"I don't know. Not as responsive to my texts. Too busy to hang out."

"He *is* a busy guy."

"Yeah, but this is different."

"And this has been going on since the party?"

"No, just the past few days."

My heart sinks. That's when I talked to Adam about Jak. I was afraid of this. It seems like he's backing off. Even though I told him to forget everything I said.

"He's probably just being an idiot," I say.

"Yeah. Whatever. I'm over it."

Unloading on Adam was selfish of me. I didn't really want him to distance himself from Jak. I don't want to cause her any distress. But . . . there's also a tiny part of me that would be glad if there were one less obstacle in our path. And that makes me feel even *more* terrible.

But Jak is either not that bothered or putting on a brave face, because she just moves right along.

"How are things with Tristen?" she asks.

It's so hard to think about Tristen when I'm with Jak. Everything I felt for Tristen in the park starts to blur.

"Things are fine," I say. "Still pretty casual."

We are definitely not still pretty casual, but if there's a sliver of truth to it, it doesn't count as a lie. How is that for rationalization?

"Life is complicated," I add.

"I heart you," Jak says.

"Wait," I say. I have to catch my breath for a moment. "Did you just say I hear you or I *heart* you?"

Jak pauses. "Uh. I think I *said* I heart you. But I meant to say I *hear* you."

Freudian slip or just honest mistake?

"Life *is* complicated," she adds.

I don't know what's happening, but here's my chance to test the romantic waters.

"Yeah," I say. "But I'd like to try to spend more time hanging out together, just the two of us."

"Totally, bro," Jak says.

Well that's not an auspicious start.

"Maybe we could do dinner one night this week," I venture.

"Okay," she says.

"There's that pizza place on Hickory I've been wanting to try."

"In."

"Or, we could get kinda fancy and go to Laredo Grill."

"That place you went to with you parents?"

"Yeah."

"Isn't it kind of romantic?"

"I guess. But it'd be fun. Just me and you. My treat."

Jak considers this.

Ask if it's a date! Ask if it's a date! Ask if it's a date!

"If it's all the same," Jak says, "I think I'd rather just stay home and order takeout in my sweatpants."

"Sure," I say, deflated. "I guess we can do that."

Jak tries to stick the entire gobstopper in her mouth.

"How do I wook?" she mumbles.

I stare at her.

She wooks like a girl I can't get out of my head.

28

TRUE TO HER CAMPAIGN promise and our conversations at both the college fair and the keg party, Rebecca fixed the administrative issue that had been causing problems in the senior parking lot. New permits were distributed, and our long national nightmare is over. I am currently headed to the lot to affix my new permit and move my car. Jak and Tristen are weighing heavily on my mind, so it feels good to be carrying out a stupid, mundane task that doesn't require considering the butterfly effect of consequences across dozens of people for generations to come.

When I cut through the faculty lot to get to my parking spot, I encounter one of the saddest things I've ever seen: Mr. Kimbrough, slumped in his reasonably priced, midsize sedan, staring into space. It looks like he's been there all day.

Mr. K. has been off the grid lately. Jak hypothesized at the keg party that Ms. Solomon had recently gotten lucky, and I chose to think positive and surmise that it was with him. Not having heard from him in a while seemed to confirm that assumption. But this sight definitely makes me think otherwise. Sigh. I feel like I joined an adopt-a-teacher program. I can't just abandon him now.

I walk up to the passenger side of his car and knock on the window. Mr. K. startles upright. He might have been sleeping, for all I know.

"Bob, are you okay?"

He rubs his bloodshot eyes and tries to play it off.

"Shane, how nice to see you. I was just working off the after-lunch snoozes."

"It's ten a.m."

"Oh. Right."

"Hold on. I'm getting in."

At this point I don't even care who sees me talking to Mr. Kimbrough. Or getting into his car, for that matter. If I can't get my own love life in order, it gives me some solace to at least help my fellow man in need.

I climb into the passenger seat. "Okay, Bob. Let me have it."

He takes a deep breath. "I've been doing everything you told me to do. Every time Deb gets a paycheck and is all smiles, I'm there."

"Great."

"After I saw you at Laredo Grill, I asked her if she uses Latisse."

"And?"

"She doesn't. But she was flattered and really impressed I even knew what it was."

"Nice."

"At the end of dinner, I insisted on paying. Like I had to get borderline aggressive."

"Gotta do what it takes."

"And then that night we kissed."

"Amazing!"

"And then a few nights later we . . . you know . . ."

"Yes!" (Side note: Jak was right!)

"And then," Mr. Kimbrough continues, "and then . . . nothing."

"What do you mean, nothing?"

"Radio silence. She avoids me at work. She doesn't pick up the phone. Nothing. I don't know what I did wrong."

I pat Mr. K. on the shoulder. I feel for the guy, I really do. Perhaps the only thing worse than getting flat-out rejected by a girl is getting a peek at the promised land and then having her slam the window shut in your face.

Mr. Kimbrough looks so downright pathetic right now, so lost, so hopeless, that I just decide . . . *what the hell, it's time for the truth.*

"Bob, I have to level with you," I say. "When you thought

I was some sort of consultant, a dating guru, a Svengali, well, you were right."

"Yeah, I mean, you've been so helpful."

"No, you don't understand. You're not the only guy I've been advising. This is like . . . a real service that I offer."

"It is?"

"Yeah. I help guys who are down on their luck win over the girls of their dreams. I try to at least even the playing field between the jocks and the have-nots. You know, I'm like . . . the Robin Hood of romance."

"I knew it!"

"It started out as kind of a hobby, but now it's become this all-consuming thing. I *did* help Adam Foster date Olivia Reyes. You were right from the beginning. I wish I had been more honest with you."

"Wow," Mr. K. says. "But I understand. I get why you would want to keep something like that a secret. Especially at this school. You kids are cruel."

"There's more," I say. "All of the tips I've been giving you, they're part of a formula I call the Galgorithm—you know, like *gal* plus *algorithm*? That's probably what you heard whispers about."

Mr. Kimbrough smirks. "Galgorithm. Huh. And people make fun of me for *my* math puns."

"You got me there," I say.

"So can I see the formula?" he asks.

"I don't think you're ready. Not yet. And besides, it's never really been used on a grown woman before. Just high school girls. But you seem like a good guy, and I wanted to help you."

"I appreciate that, Shane. Everything you've done for me." He exhales. "I guess you can file me under lost causes."

"Well, not so fast. You never know. Is Deb teaching right now?"

Mr. Kimbrough checks the time on his phone. "No. She's off."

"Okay, let's text her."

"I'm telling you, she won't respond."

"Let's try the Galgorithm."

Mr. K. considers it, then relents and picks up his phone.

"Try writing: 'Can you pick up the tickets at will call?'"

"Huh?" Mr. K. says. "What tickets?"

"Just try it."

"Okay . . ." He sends her the text.

A moment later he gets a response.

"Holy cow, she wrote back!" he says.

"See?" I say. "There's hope. What did she write?"

"She wrote, 'Did you mean to send this to me?'"

"Perfect," I say. "We just needed a breezy nonsense text to get her to reply. Now let's engage her. Write: 'Sorry. I sent that to the wrong person. How are you?'"

He sends the text. Now Mr. Kimbrough is sitting on the edge of the driver's seat.

She writes back immediately, and he shows me the text: *Good, u??*

"Two question marks and a comma," I say. "That's a great sign. Now write: 'It's been a long week..' Make sure to put two dots at the end."

"Why two dots?"

"It's more than a period but less than an ellipsis. It makes you seem intriguing."

He types it.

"Shane, this is unbelievable. You need to be charging for this."

"I do it for the love," I say.

She writes back again, and Mr. Kimbrough reads it out loud: "'Same here.'"

And then a second text in quick succession: "'It's so hot today.' But instead of 'hot' it's a little picture of a fire."

"Good cadence on her replies," I say. "Great pace. And she sent two texts in a row. *And* she used an emoji. All excellent signs."

Mr. Kimbrough looks at me like I just discovered the atom.

"Let's take a shot downfield," I say. "Write: 'Beers?'"

Mr. Kimbrough types and sends as fast as he possibly can. And then . . . nothing.

"What happened?" he asks.

"Just give it a minute."

A minute goes by. No response.

"I'll just write, 'Maybe another time.'"

"No!" I say, and actually slap his hand. "Never write two texts in a row. Two texts in a row demonstrates weakness. We're not weak. We're strong."

Mr. Kimbrough pulls his fingers off the keyboard.

"Wait a second," I say.

Waiting . . . waiting . . . waiting . . . and then a *ping* that she's responded! Me and Bob cheer in his car in the middle of the parking lot like we just won the Super Bowl.

Our glee is short-lived, though. "She wrote: 'Don't think I'm up for beers.'"

Mr. Kimbrough is immediately discouraged. I'm not.

"Write back: 'LOL. Didn't even write that. One of the kids grabbed my phone. #brats.'"

Mr. Kimbrough looks at me.

"You can use that as a believable mulligan like once a year."

He shakes his head incredulously and sends the text.

She responds quickly and he shows me: *OMG. Totallyyy. These kids are a pain in my neck ;)*

"Good," I say. "Now shut your phone off."

"What? Why?"

"You got an acronym, a triple consonant, and an old school emoticon. You hit the jackpot."

"So shouldn't I write back?"

"Nope. Not now at least. You're in a good spot. Always let

her send the last text. It shows poise and keeps her on her toes."

"Genius," Mr. Kimbrough says, as he dutifully shuts his phone off.

"You're back in the mix with Deb," I say. "I'm not sure what happened before, but things should start to flow now. I can also give you a few more pointers later. And there are some rules you need to follow if we're gonna be working together officially. But that's enough for today."

Mr. Kimbrough sits back in his seat and looks up at the roof, relieved.

Cyrano has nothing on me.

29

STUDENT GOVERNMENT IS just a few doors down from anime club but has much more luxurious digs, meeting in an extra-large conference room with a lectern, a gavel, and a whiteboard. It's from this lectern, with said gavel, that Rebecca, as Student Council president, wields influence.

Rebecca and Adam have also been using this room to finalize their proposal for a second extra period after school. They posted fliers around the hallways promoting the idea and announcing an "open meeting," which they are hosting together, to discuss it and seek approval. Approval from who, as Tristen would say, or *whom*, as Jak would say, I have no idea. It's really the nerdiest idea ever, and one they'll only get to enjoy for a couple more months anyway. But you know these overachieving types, always trying to leave a legacy.

I haven't come to the open meeting to check on their progress, though. No, after hearing some pretty unbelievable chitchat in the halls, I've come here to see if Rebecca and Adam are hooking up.

When I told Adam what I was feeling, or thought I was feeling, for Jak, I never meant to come between them. At least not explicitly. But that's exactly what happened, and I should have seen it coming. According to the dribbles of information I get from Jak, Adam has remained aloof. Making matters worse is Jak herself, who is ambivalent on her best day and standoffish on her worst, and has not made much of an effort to show Adam she's still interested.

When I first heard gossip about Adam and Rebecca, I dismissed it out of hand. But the more I thought about it, the more it made sense. They *have* been spending a lot of time together. And they do have a lot in common, considering they both already have two-page resumes. Sure, Rebecca is a put-together prep and Adam is a disheveled doofus, but he learned enough from me to win over Olivia and charm Jak, so it's not out of the realm of possibility that he could succeed a third time.

When I open the door to the student-government office, Rebecca and Adam are standing at the conference table. Rebecca is wearing a fashionable gray button-down, and Adam looks like he robbed a big and tall store under the cover of darkness. But together they pass for the cliché version of an illicit office romance: sleeves rolled up, hands accidentally touching over a stack of paperwork. I half expect Adam to sweep everything off the desk and take Rebecca right there in front of me.

Alas, they just greet me warmly and invite me inside. I'm not surprised that I'm the only one who bothered to show up for this thing.

"How's it going, guys?" I ask innocently.

"Pretty good so far," Adam says.

"What do you think about these names for the extra period, Shane?" Rebecca asks. "Extra Extracurricular, Double Extracurricular, or ECX, which stands for Extracurricular Extreme."

"Definitely ECX."

"See, I told you," Adam says to Rebecca. "Your idea is the best."

"You're sweet," Rebecca says, and brushes his shoulder with her hand.

I can't confirm that something is happening between them, but something is definitely not *not* happening. The whole thing makes me kind of squeamish. I feel bad for Jak. I need to get out of here.

I am starting to offer hasty goodbyes and retreat when Rebecca suddenly gasps.

"What's wrong?" I ask.

"Get out of here!" she yells.

At first I think she's yelling at me. But then I spin around and realize she's talking to Harrison, who has appeared in the doorway behind me.

"Hi, Rebecca," he says.

Rebecca shakes her head. "Not now, Harrison. I can't do this."

"What's going on?" Adam asks.

No one responds. I'm willing to bet that Adam still doesn't know about Rebecca and Harrison's history.

"Is he the problem?" Harrison asks, as he enters the room. I can see he's clutching one of the fliers advertising the open meeting. "Is he why you won't return my texts? Why do I have to track you down like this?"

"He has nothing to do with this!" Rebecca says.

The "he" Harrison is referring to is me. Not Adam, who is standing *shoulder to shoulder* with Rebecca, but me, who is standing across the table.

"I'm not doing anything!" I insist.

"You better shut up, dude," Harrison says to me. There's only five feet of space between us.

"Um, am I missing something?" Adam asks.

"Harrison," Rebecca says calmly, "you know as well as I do that we're not dating anymore because of your temper and your need to sneak around. I've had enough. I want someone stable, who can be my partner. In public."

She places her hand on top of Adam's on the desk.

"Wait, you guys used to date?" Adam says.

All of a sudden Harrison steps to me, grabs me by the front of my collar, and pushes me against the wall of the room.

"Harrison, stop!" Rebecca pleads.

Adam doesn't move.

Harrison cocks his fist back to punch me. I recoil in fear.

"Harrison," I plead. "Lemme go!"

Harrison keeps his fist cocked and considers his options. He's not making any sense. I wish I could get inside his head and see how he ticks. Probably like a time bomb.

"What's going on in here? Let go of him!"

Harrison freezes. We both look up. It's Ms. Solomon. Yes, Deb, who also happens to be the student-government faculty advisor, and who has just entered the room to play savior.

Harrison sneers at this missed opportunity, lets go of my collar, and even straightens it out a bit. "Just fooling around," he says to Ms. Solomon. "Right, Shane?"

He glares at me. "Right," I mumble.

"Everyone out except student-government participants!" Ms. Solomon says. "I don't want to see any more horsing around!" She points at the door.

But the doorway is now blocked—by Tristen.

Harrison continues anyway, nearly bumping into her once again. They barely acknowledge each other, and then Harrison slips by and exits.

I take a moment to breathe.

"Out!" Deb says to me.

"Come on, Tristen," I say.

I grab her by the hand and pull her out of the room. Harrison is already halfway down the hall by the time we exit, and then he takes the stairs to another floor. Deb closes the door behind us. It's now just me and Tristen in the hallway alone.

My head is spinning, metaphorically and literally. I'm dizzy.

"Are you okay, Shane?" Tristen asks. "You're all red. What happened to your collar?" She must have just missed the action.

"What? Yeah. I'm fine. How did you know I was in there?"

"I didn't. But I saw Adam's name on some fliers and I figured I would ask him where you were. I messaged you, I tweeted you, I sent you like a million snaps."

"I'm sorry," I say. "It's been a crazy week."

Since our rendezvous in the park I've been trying to slow things down with Tristen. Just long enough to clear my head and reconcile my feelings for Jak.

"You want to come over to my house tonight and watch a movie?" she asks. "My parents will be home, but they'll let me keep the door closed."

I hesitate.

A growing chorus inside my head is telling me to just go with it. When in my life will a girl like Tristen be this obsessed with me? Things with Jak have gone nowhere. Why am I putting myself through all this?

"Just come over," Tristen says. "I have new brochures from that save the dolphins organization I want to show you. They're so cute! Just like you!"

She takes my hand. I consider the sordid game I'm playing between Tristen and Jak and Adam and Rebecca and Harrison. Like those dolphins, I've entered into dangerous territory. The question is, who will be there to save me?

30

"HERE YOU GO," JAK SAYS as she tosses my Fitbit at me. "You think just because you were all sweet and helped me when I was drunk you could get out of this? Nuh uh. Besides, they're waterproof. You didn't even need to take them off."

We're sitting at Jak's kitchen table, and she's returning the Fitbit I left in her bathroom when I took her home from the party.

"I charged them and everything," she says.

She slips hers back on her wrist and I do the same.

Jak's kitchen is rustic and eclectic—wooden table and chairs and purposefully mismatched place mats and utensils. Too many containers of Chinese takeout sit in front of us. We've been slowly but surely working our way through them. Jak is wearing sweatpants, as promised.

"I'm not gonna lie," I say. "I thought the step competition was over."

"Never."

"Well, do the steps I took while carrying you home count as double?"

"Touché, Chambliss. Touché."

It's been a rocky couple of weeks since the keg party, but I think things with Jak are finally getting back to normal. We've returned to the rhythms of joking and poking fun that have made our friendship special from the beginning. I don't know if I will ever be able to look at her the same way I did before I saw her soaking wet and half-naked, but I've begun to realize there is no way to further explore my feelings for her without actually telling her about them. And that's just not something I'm willing to do. It's too risky. Those are words I can't take back.

"By the way," Jak says, "have you heard about Adam?"

"Uh, what about him?"

"Supposedly he's seeing Rebecca Larabie."

"Oh, yeah. I guess I heard something about that."

"I thought she was dating Harrison."

"No, that's definitely over."

"Oh."

"Are you upset?"

"Nah," Jak says. "I did like Adam. But we only hung out a few times. It is what it is. He sent me a nice text the other day, just saying hello."

I could have talked to Adam as soon as I realized he was backing off from Jak. But Jak never really seemed very broken up about it, as near as I could tell, so I figured why get myself further involved? And now Adam and Rebecca are together, and Jak is . . . well, now Jak is available. Theoretically.

"At least I can officially cross Adam off my list of potential prom dates," Jak says.

Prom. It's barely even been on my radar.

"*You* have a list of potential dates?" I say. "You never talk about prom. I thought you said it was . . . what do you always say it is?"

"Part of the prom-industrial complex."

"Right, that."

"Yeah, well, it *is* super lame," she says. "But I want to go anyway just to prove to everyone how lame it is."

"Yeah that'll show 'em."

"What's going on with Tristen? Now *she* could fill out a dress."

"Status quo."

"I don't know what that means."

"It means the same."

"Are you kidding me, Chambliss? I'm in the ninety-ninth percentile of all English students. I know what 'status quo' means."

She flicks an unopened soy sauce packet at me. I let it hit me in the cheek and fall onto my plate.

"You have superlative reflexes," she says, before adding, "That means *good*."

Jak smiles at her own cleverness. She takes out some ChapStick and applies it.

"What kind is that?" I venture.

She shrugs. "I don't know. The black tube is just regular, I guess. I like it 'cause it's the same kind my dad uses. When I use it it's like getting a kiss from my dad!"

Well, that didn't go in the direction I was hoping.

She puts some more on. "Why?"

"No reason. Just curious."

"Which kind do you use?"

"You know I use the blue tube, with moisturizer."

"Eww, blue is the worst. It tastes like cough medicine."

"Well, then you can't have any of mine."

Jak shrugs and goes back to eating.

When I used ChapStick to lay groundwork for future physicality with Tristen, it went so smoothly, unlike this. I'm reminded of the conversation I had with Jak in the cafeteria, when she was making fun of me for not being able to take off her bra. Even though we were joking, that was a pretty racy topic. Is it possible that, in her own way, *Jak* was laying groundwork for future physicality with *me*? Or am I just grasping at straws and bra straps?

The Galgorithm has been wearing on me lately. Guys constantly expecting advice and direction. It's a grind. I don't have all the answers. And that's never been truer than right now, when I'm desperately trying to use my "expertise" in my own life.

"Jak," I say, "you know what I never noticed about you before? Your eyelashes. They're so long."

"My eyelashes?" she says, and instinctively bats her eyes.

"Yeah."

Jak thinks about this. Probably for the first time in her life, she is silent for more than fifteen seconds.

Finally she says: "My eyelashes are the *worst*. They're so short and dry. And I think they have split ends, which I didn't even know was possible. Like, how can you have split eyelashes? It's probably because I always forget to wash my face."

She goes back to eating. "Why are you even looking at my eyelashes? Stalker."

So much for that.

Whatever I may feel for Jak, it's pretty obvious she doesn't feel the same way about me. I'm sick of being confused, and I'm fed up with carrying the burden of everyone else's dating issues on my shoulders to boot. AP exams are approaching. And then finals and then prom and then graduation and then summer and then college. It's all happening too fast. Something's gotta change between now and then. Before *everything* changes.

31

I'VE ALWAYS SAID THAT one day Reed Wanamaker could be president of the United States. He could own a yacht. He could host a beauty pageant. He could do all those things if he only saw the potential in himself that I see in him.

Now the rest of the world finally sees that potential.

It didn't surprise me much when Reed dropped off the face of the earth. After he made out with Marisol in the courtyard of the school in broad daylight, there was nothing more I could do for him. He was my masterpiece, and he had leveled up.

But Reed was always a good friend, and devoted to the cause, so when I made the momentous decision that I made today, I knew I had to seek him out.

I find him in the gym during his phys ed period. Both basketball courts are full of students running drills. The air is filled with the sound of dribbling balls and sneaker squeaks and the smell of Spalding rubber.

Reed, however, is not participating and is instead standing on the sidelines in street clothes, intently playing with his iPhone. Those street clothes, it's worth noting, are pretty stylish and a complete departure from the outfits he wore when we first met, though he hasn't added a pound to his skeletal frame.

"There's the man," I say as I approach him.

"Shane!" He pockets the phone and hugs me.

"Wait," I say. "Why aren't you playing? Are you sick?"

"Nope." He shrugs nonchalantly. "Just didn't feel like it."

The new and improved Reed has swagger!

We sit in a couple of stray folding chairs that are next to the court.

"It's been a little while," I say. "I feel like I never got the nitty-gritty."

"I know. Things have just gotten so busy with school and SATs . . . and Marisol."

He motions to the basketball court, where Marisol is chatting with a bunch of her friends. She blows Reed a kiss. This is of course the class where they first met. And to think she'll never even know I was behind it. There's something poetic about that.

"Well, you did text me that you were officially a couple," I say.

Reed smiles.

"I'm happy for you, man," I add.

"I can't thank you enough, Shane. You changed my life. All the pointers. All the advice."

"Hey, it was in you the whole time. You really went for it that day in the courtyard."

"I don't know what came over me," he says. "Maybe it was just sixteen years of frustration. But Marisol was laughing at my jokes and it was a beautiful day outside and suddenly I didn't care anymore. I just kissed her. And she kissed me back! Everything clicked. We've been together ever since. I guess when it's right it's right."

I pat Reed on the back. I almost want to cry I'm so proud.

"Thanks for letting me make fun of you in front of Tristen," he adds. "I felt bad about that."

"Yeah, she didn't care." I can't seem to do any wrong in Tristen's eyes.

"Phew. Good," he says. "So did you just come here to say hey or what?"

"No," I say. "Actually, there's something I wanted to talk to you about."

"Is everything okay?"

"Yeah. It's just . . . well, I'm really glad you were one of my final clients, Reed."

"The pleasure was all mine. Wait—what do you mean, *final* clients?"

"I thought you should be the first to know."

"First to know what?"

"I'm retiring from the dating business."

"You mean like when you graduate?"

"No, I mean right now. I'm done. No more coaching. No more advising. No more telling guys what to say. No more hearing their sob stories. I'm finished."

"You're joking."

"Dead serious. I'm gonna start reaching out to my clients to let them know I'm through. I've taken them as far as I can anyway."

"I don't understand," Reed says.

The fact is, my mental state is beginning to fray. The trials and tribulations of one budding relationship are plenty to keep anyone occupied around the clock. But facilitating multiple relationships at once? It's enough to drive a guy insane. And how can I be a dating expert when I can't even get my own house in order? I used to be passionate about helping guys find true love. Now it just reminds me what I lack in my own life.

"It's better this way," is all I say. "It's time."

"I just . . . I can't believe it," Reed says. "I always thought you would do this forever."

"I used to think so too. But it wears on you. I'm ready to move on. I think I've contributed enough. And I hoped you of all people would understand that."

"Of course. I absolutely do. It's just . . ."

"It's just what?"

"It's just . . . what about the Galgorithm?"

"What about it?"

"What's gonna happen to it? Are you ever gonna share it?"

"I think maybe it's better if it stays a secret forever."

"Come on, Shane! You have to tell me."

"You really want to know?"

"Yes!"

"And you promise not to tell anyone else?"

"Yes!"

I take a deep breath. Here goes.

"Well, Reed, the truth is . . . the Galgorithm doesn't exist."

"What do you mean, it doesn't exist?"

"I mean, there's no such thing as the Galgorithm. I made it up."

He's silent. Words replaced by background sounds of basketball and gossip.

"But—"

I cut him off. "No. No code. No formula. No Galgorithm. It's not real."

"But I've asked you before what it was," he says.

"And every time I told you that you weren't ready to hear the truth yet. The thing is, you'll never be ready, because there's no secret to reveal."

"Then why did you tell me there was one!"

"To gain your trust."

"I don't get it."

"I've spent years trying to observe and learn everything I could about girls and couples and relationships. All the moves and the techniques I shared with you, those were all real. But for guys like you to truly get on board, I needed you to think everything was part of a master plan. So I started calling my wisdom the Galgorithm."

Reed is speechless.

"Look, every girl is different. There's no singular formula. Guys are just much more willing to go along with the program if they believe there is one. The Galgorithm was just me telling you what to do next."

"But it really did seem like there *was* a code," Reed says. "Like it *worked*."

"That's because it did work. By distracting you."

"What do you mean?"

"At the end of the day, all that matters is confidence. That's the one common denominator I found in every guy who is successful with women. It doesn't matter if you're tall or a jock or good-looking or rich. But the problem is, confidence is not a thing. You can't see it. You can't measure it. You can't buy it. You can't just tell a guy, 'Be more confident.' But what you can do, I discovered, is create the *illusion* of confidence."

The wheels are turning in Reed's head.

"By pumping you up with all these rules and tricks, and by

making you think you were following a formula, I distracted you from fixating on how ungettable the girl standing in front of you seemed. I made you less nervous. And that made you more confident."

I think about Mr. Kimbrough, reluctant to try to text Deb again—that is, until I told him we were using "the Galgorithm."

"I didn't even know any of this was happening," Reed says.

"Exactly. Because you were thinking about your haircut and the jeans and how long to wait to text her back and how much cologne to put on and *what is the Galgorithm?* It's a decoy. Figuring out that Marisol likes pizza from her Facebook profile wasn't rocket science. But convincing you that the intel was invaluable—now, *that* was what made your conversation with her less daunting. When you think you have the Galgorithm behind you, guiding you, you're much more confident, and it shows."

I think about Adam putting a pen behind his ear and then asking Olivia—and Jak—for another one. Simply a ruse to distract him from the fact that he was approaching a girl he considered out of his league. Otherwise he would have overthought it and psyched himself out.

"My brain is throbbing right now," Reed says. "So there's no spreadsheet? No hieroglyphics carved into a rock somewhere?"

"Let me ask you this, Reed: Did you ever *really* believe that I had unlocked the mystery of girls?"

"Well, I was vulnerable. I would have believed anything at that point. And then it worked, so . . . I would have to say, yes. I did believe you. Or at least I chose not to *not* believe you."

"Yeah, that's pretty much how it works."

"So all those tips and hints . . ."

"In here," I say, pointing to my head. "I *am* the Galgorithm."

"But you're done."

"That's right. So I guess, in a way, I'm destroying it by retiring. The Galgorithm is gone."

"It seems like such a waste."

"Yeah, well, you have Marisol and I have . . ." I trail off. What do I have?

The bell rings for the end of class.

"Hey, Reed," I say. "Let's just keep this between me and you for now."

"Of course," he says. "I'm still trying to digest it all."

We stand up. Reed digs his phone out of his pocket. "Thanks for telling me," he says. "I really appreciate it." We hug.

"I'll see you around, Reed. Good luck."

"You too, Shane."

I'm proud of what we accomplished together. I'm proud of the man he's become.

Reed turns and leaves, but as soon as he does, I notice he

is immediately engrossed by his phone again, in a not-even-normal-for-a-high-school-kid kind of way.

"Hey," I call out. "What are you doing over there?"

He scurries back to me sheepishly so that no one else can hear us and shows me an app on his phone.

"I'm playing Dungeons and Dragons. Don't tell Marisol."

I shake my head with pride.

Some nerds never change.

32

I'M ENJOYING MY FIRST day of freedom in a long time.

I'm surprised by how good it feels to have this weight off my shoulders. I woke up this morning with no clients to check up on and no advice to dole out. There are a handful of guys that I do still need to inform about my retirement, but that's a task for another day.

As soon as I left for school in the morning, I knew I wasn't actually gonna go. I need a break. I deserve it. And I'm prepared for my upcoming AP exams. I left the house at the proper time so that my parents wouldn't suspect anything, but as soon as I was a block away, I changed direction and started driving to the mall. Not exactly *Ferris Bueller's Day Off*, but it's a start.

My phone pings. It's Jak. The texts begin around this

time every morning and continue until she falls asleep. They are usually entertaining, but today they start to eat away at that nice feeling of relief, so I just shut my phone off.

There's only one thing at the mall open this early, a diner that's accessible from the street. It's a real greasy spoon, and the waitresses are dressed liked it's the fifties. I order black coffee with my breakfast. I never drink black coffee. But it seems like what a normal, soon-to-be-collegiate guy would do. It's bitter as hell. I have two cups and get a third to go.

When the rest of the mall finally opens, I wander about aimlessly, past stores I've browsed with Reed or Tristen or Jak. This time I have the place pretty much to myself. I pass a trendy women's boutique. There's one girl shopping in the store, and she looks cute. She's about fifteen feet away from me, and I can only see her from behind. I pause to look at her.

I start to take another step but can't keep my eyes off her. Her hair is long and jet black. She fiddles with it while she browses a rack of shirts.

I'm struck with a sudden sense of déjà vu, but my brain can't yet articulate what's happening.

Time slows to a crawl.

The girl takes a hair tie off her wrist and puts her hair in a bun.

She has a bar code tattoo on the back of her neck.

I drop my cup.

Voldemort.

The coffee splatters all over the floor and my sneakers, and echoes in the concourse loud enough for her to hear.

She turns and spots me, and her face lights up.

"Shane!" she says, and immediately stops what she was doing and walks in my direction. My stomach drops.

When we dated, she was a sixteen-year-old high school junior, and that's how I remember her. Now she's a nineteen-year-old college sophomore, and the years have been very kind to her. Her hair is dyed black, but she's still rocking that red lipstick and nail polish. Any trace of a baby face is gone. Those two perfect dimples are now accenting a pair of taut cheekbones. She wears a white off-the-shoulder T-shirt and black jeans, and she looks damn good.

Luckily, the coffee was half empty. I quickly wipe off my sneakers with a napkin and throw the spilled cup in a nearby garbage can just as Voldemort reaches me.

"This is so crazy!" she says. She gives me a big hug. I hug her back. She smells the same. Our entire relationship flashes before my eyes. It doesn't take very long.

"Faith," I stammer. "What are you doing here?"

"I have reading days, so I decided to visit my folks."

"Reading days?"

"We get a couple of days off before finals start. I should be studying, but I decided to come home. The mall in Valley Hills sucks, though."

"Got it," I manage.

My synapses are overrun. I hate her. I'm happy to see her. I'm shocked. I'm curious. I'm upset. I'm weak.

"So," she says, "it's been forever. How have you been? What have you been up to?"

Oh, just obsessing over our breakup until it metastasized into the creation of a new identity for myself. You know, silly high school stuff.

"Not much," I say. "Looking forward to graduation and whatever."

"Right on," she says. "Well you look great. Something is different about you."

She's gonna mention my jeans. . . .

"New jeans?"

"Yeah." I try to play it off. "I think so."

"They look good. Hey . . . shouldn't you be at school?"

"Nah. I decided to cut a few periods."

"Senioritis. Nice. I remember it well."

We've exhausted our supply of pleasantries. She bites her lower lip. Still gets me after all these years.

"Well, it was great to see you, Shane. Such a happy coincidence."

"You too."

"I'm gonna take off. I should probably actually do a little studying."

She hugs me again. My hand grazes her bare shoulder.

It's weird; I never thought our skin would ever touch again.

"Take care," she says.

She's about to turn and leave.

"Faith, wait."

She stops and looks at me expectantly.

I'm five inches taller than her, but I feel so small.

"Um," I manage. "I have to ask . . ."

If I don't, I will regret it for the rest of my life. But I can't get the goddamn words out. I'm so flustered.

"Us . . . ," I say.

She nods her head. She understands. Of course she does.

"What happened between us, you mean."

"Yeah," I say. "I feel like . . . you never told me why."

"Why we broke up? A lot of reasons," she says. "And also no reason."

Dating Faith was certainly a whirlwind. She took a shine to me, and I just got swept up in it. Back then I had no clue. I was ill-equipped to handle a girlfriend, let alone an older one. But the abruptness with which Faith ended things still vexes me.

"I mean," she continues, "you were young. A little immature. We both were. I guess . . . it was clear it was much more serious for you than it was for me. I just wanted to have fun, you know?"

"So it wasn't like I did anything or said anything or something like that?"

"No, not at all," she says. "I mean, not that I can remember. It was like forever ago already."

Yeah, forever ago.

"You aren't still upset about it, are you?" she asks.

"No," I lie. "It's just . . . you know. It sucked."

"I know," she says. "I feel bad. But some things just aren't meant to be. And you can't force it. Trust me, you're gonna have a lot of relationships. And not every one is gonna be perfect. You just have to go with it sometimes."

"Easier said than done."

"Life is easier said than done, Shane."

"That's true" is all I mutter.

"What about now?" she asks. "Any girls in your life?"

A loaded question if there ever was one.

"Yeah." I waver. "I don't know."

"Hmm," she says. "Funny, I totally would have guessed you would've gotten together with Jak by now."

I blink.

"What did you say?"

"Jak. I met her a few times when we were hanging out."

"I know, but why would you think we would have gotten together?"

"Um, because you're, like, so obviously in love with her."

I go slack-jawed.

"Jak?"

"Yes, Jak." She laughs. "You talked about her all the time.

Like, in front of me. Like, rudely in front of me. I've never seen two people more clearly in love."

I'm dazed. I feel like there are cartoon birds flying around my head.

"You're totally perfect for each other," she continues. "Literally everyone in the world knows that except for you."

"But she's my best friend."

"Duh. You think people want to date their worst enemy?"

I feel a little woozy.

Of course.

How could I have been such an idiot?

This is what I've been feeling the whole time!

Jak knows me better than anyone and she *still* sticks around.

I feel lost when she's not by my side.

I'm her soul mate.

And she's mine.

I'm in love with Jak.

I'm in love with Jak!

"Shane? Hello?" Faith asks. "Are you okay?"

"You're right," I say finally. "I . . . just . . . can't believe how stupid I am. Of course I'm in love with Jak!"

There. I said it.

Faith sighs and grins. "Boys. You are so dumb."

"I'm in love with Jak," I say again, still processing.

"That's a good start," Faith says. "But the question is, does Jak know?"

I shake my head no.

"Well, luckily, you know where to find her."

"Where?" I ask eagerly.

"School, probably."

"Oh, right."

I've not only lost track of time, but also the space-time continuum.

"You should go," she says.

"Okay. I'm going."

"Good luck, Shane. It was nice to see you."

"Thanks, Vo—"

She looks at me quizzically.

I correct myself. "Faith."

And then I turn and run.

33

MY HEART IS POUNDING, and it's not the two and half cups of black coffee.

I peel into my parking spot at school. I park over the lines in two places, but I don't care. All I can think about is getting inside to talk to Jak.

I ran from Faith to my car in the parking lot at the mall, and now I'm running from my car toward school and toward Jak. I smile to myself, thinking about how many Fitbit steps I've already racked up today on the way to this grand gesture.

I knew I felt something deep in my gut when I spent half the night in Jak's bathtub nursing her back to sobriety. But maybe my subconscious was protecting me from realizing the truth. There were so many obstacles that would have prevented us from getting together: our friendship, Adam,

Tristen, the pledge Jak swore to remain platonic after Faith left me heartbroken.

Tristen certainly remains an issue, but my feelings for her are complicated. I do care about her. Just . . . not in the way I care about Jak. I'm not in love with Tristen. I'm in love with Jak. *I'm in love with Jak!* I have to end things with Tristen. I don't know how she'll take it, but I can't even think about that right now. No, all that's important right now is proclaiming my true love to Jak and convincing her that it will not only preserve our friendship, but also strengthen it.

I enter school through a side door that is just off the senior hallway, the quicker to get to Jak's locker. As soon as I take a step inside, though, I can tell something is wrong. There's a buzz in the hallway. Lots of whispering and giggling. At first I think it's just the Kingsview rumor mill being kicked into overdrive by some silly hookup gossip. But as I get closer to Jak's locker, I start to realize that things are very, very wrong. My classmates are staring. Those whispers, those giggles, they're directed *at me*.

My heart beats even faster. I rack my brain for any possible reason why I am suddenly the center of attention. I remember I turned off my phone hours ago, so I pull it out of my pocket and turn it back on. I get to Jak's locker, but she's not there, which is odd. I know her schedule down to the second. I look at my phone: dozens of texts and e-mails and missed calls from my clients, but nothing recent from Jak. That's weird.

Everyone around me is snickering. *What the hell is going on?*

I notice that several onlookers are holding today's edition of the *Kingsview Chronicle,* which is also kinda odd because the paper is usually cafeteria or bathroom reading, not water-cooler fodder. I find a copy on the floor a few steps from Jak's locker. Kids are Snapchatting pictures of me and laughing as I pick it up. WTF?

I open the paper and feel like I am having an out-of-body experience. I cannot believe my eyes. The banner headline reads:

GALGORITHM: A DATING GURU
AND HIS SECRET FORMULA

This cannot be happening. This. Cannot. Be happening. I read the first couple of lines:

> *In a shocking* Chronicle *exclusive, senior*
> *Shane Chambliss has been exposed as the*
> *resident dating doctor at Kingsview High*
> *School, boasting a roster of unlucky-in-*
> *love classmates and a powerful algorithm*
> *he claims will attract female students.*
> *The scheme was first discovered when it*
> *was referenced on math teacher Robert*
> *Kimbrough's personal blog . . .*

Nooooooooooo!

I'm having trouble breathing. What? How? Mr. K., what the hell did you do?

I look at the byline of the article. It was written by . . . Brooke Nast? You've got to be kidding me. *Balloon?*

I pull out my phone again and launch the browser. *No service.* Goddamn it!

With all eyes on me, and still holding the paper, I sprint toward the computer lab down the hall. I've never run so much in one day in my life. I make a hard left and burst into the lab. Thankfully, the room is empty.

There are five rows of computers, all relatively new iMac desktops. I sit at the terminal closest to the door and log in with my Kingsview High ID. I google Mr. Kimbrough's Humble Pi blog. I curse the stupid caricature of him when it loads. Most of the entries are just random ruminations and *xkcd*-esque cartoons. Then I get about ten posts down, and my jaw drops.

If I'm reading this correctly . . .

It can't be.

It is.

Mr. Kimbrough has created an *actual* Galgorithm.

Under the misleadingly academic and, I'm assuming, tongue-in-cheek heading "A Mathematical Look at Conversing with Women," he's taken all the texting tips I've given him, formatted them into an Excel spreadsheet, and created a *real algorithm* that analyzes text messages from girls.

It's actually pretty sophisticated, and I'm starting to go numb trying to decipher it, but I eventually figure out that there are five variables in the formula: *pace* (how quickly she responds and how frequently), *cadence* (if she sends multiple texts in a row and who sent the last text), *punctuation* (use of commas, exclamation points, and question marks), *shorthand* (use of acronyms, emojis, and emoticons), and *format* (repeating of vowels, repeating of consonants, and capitalization). Each variable is calculated separately using its own individual formula, and then all the factors are weighted by statistical significance and added together, revealing in one final number—concludes the post—exactly how interested in you a woman is based on her texts.

It's mad. It's genius. It's scary. And the subtitle reads "Galgorithm—courtesy of Anonymous."

If Mr. Kimbrough didn't name names, then how the hell did it get linked to me?

To make matters much, much worse, beneath the spreadsheet are some of the tips and techniques I've been periodically doling out to Mr. Kimbrough over the past few months. Only he calls them "Corollaries to the Galgorithm," has given some of them overly fancy technical names, and follows each one with a detailed explanation.

- Social media initiation window
- Blind carbon copy trapdoor method
- Female Pavlovian response mechanism
- Prejection avoidance and warning signs
- Nonsense text beachhead establishment
- Two-dot ellipsis/period hybrid character
- Laying groundwork for future physicality
- Eyelash fail-safe with Latisse modification
- Cloud-based fragrance application strategy

This doesn't sound like advice on talking to women; it sounds like instructions for installing new enterprise software or launching a counterterrorism offensive.

I think I'm gonna have a panic attack. At the very bottom of the post is a crude visitor counter. It reads 15,014.

I look at the school paper again. Brooke has taken all of this nonsense from the blog and attributed it to me in far-from-flattering fashion.

I've been outed.

Before I can even figure out what to do next, the door to the computer lab opens, and Mr. Kimbrough himself rushes in. He looks distressed. So I can only imagine what I look like.

I glare at him. He puts his hands up as if he comes in peace.

"Some students told me you were in here. Are you okay?"

"Bob, what the hell is this? *What did you do?*"

"I was just messing around, and I decided to take all the advice you gave me and . . . see if I could reverse-engineer the formula. It was just a goof."

"A goof? A *goof*? Bob, this is insane!"

"I didn't mean for everyone to see it. It was just for a few of my nerdy math-teacher friends who read my blog. It's supposed to be a joke. I didn't even put your name on it."

"Then why the hell is my name all over the front page of the paper!"

"I don't know! I swear!"

"This article makes me look like some kind of freak!"

"Now, Shane, just take it easy. We'll figure this out."

I look back at the computer screen, as well as the newspaper. This feels like it isn't real, like it's some kind of nightmare.

"You have to delete this!" I say.

"It's too late. It's already been duplicated on the *Chronicle* website and God knows where else. If I delete it now, it will only make things worse."

"Goddamn it, Bob. You *do* know this isn't right, right? You can't put girls into a formula. You can't predict what they're gonna do. They're *girls*. This is creepy!"

"But *you* have a formula, Shane."

"*It's not real!* There's no such thing as the Galgorithm! It was just a ploy to bolster your confidence, to get you to believe in yourself and listen to my advice! Which, by the way, I'm not even giving out anymore. I'm done with the whole thing.

I gave it up. I'm being humiliated for something that doesn't even exist! People are gonna think I'm some kind of insane stalker!"

"I'm so sorry, Shane. I don't know what to say. I don't know how it got out. I posted this stuff weeks ago, and no one even said anything. It had twenty-six views the last time I checked."

I rub my temples and run my hands through my hair.

"This can't be happening."

"I'm sorry," Bob repeats. "I didn't mean for any of this. The *Chronicle* picked it up and it just went viral. I only found out this morn—oh no. Deb! Deb is gonna see this!" Bob suddenly gets lost in his own thoughts.

But I don't have any time to deal with his problems. I have to get to Balloon!

I jump up from my seat, but then stop for a moment to shake my head.

"Bob, you were supposed to deny till you die!"

34

I BRAVE MORE HALLWAYS full of leering classmates. Everyone loves a scandal, especially cruel and hormonal high school kids. The article in the *Chronicle* not only makes me look like a creep who has reduced girls to a formula and gives his pickup lines military-grade nicknames, but also a puppet master who is deviously pulling the strings behind the Kingsview dating scene. It's a total hatchet job.

There's detail and dirt in the article that didn't come from Humble Pi, though, including my identity, so Balloon better be able to shed some light on what the hell is going on, and fast.

I manage to make it to the newspaper office, which is in the administration hallway between Student Council and Model UN. Fake government, fake diplomacy, and now fake news.

I've never actually been inside the *Chronicle*'s offices

before and for some reason half expect it to be filled with whirring, steampunk-style printing presses. Instead it's just a bunch of desks arranged in bullpens. Oh, and there's a giant map of the world tacked to a bulletin board, laughably implying that anyone here really cares about what happens outside the stucco towers of Kingsview.

When I walk in, everyone in the room stops what they're doing and stares at me. I ignore them and zero in on Brooke, who is standing in an alcove in the back, talking to another student. I figure she's been in the office all day, moderating the sure-to-be-entertaining comments section for the story on the newspaper's website. When Brooke sees me, she sends the other kid on his way. I approach her. Cute, bubbly, cherubic Balloon is actually the devil in disguise.

"What the hell, Brooke?"

I can tell she's been preparing for this confrontation.

"I could say the same thing to you, Shane."

"You have to retract this story. Or delete it."

"Why would I do that?"

"Because it misrepresents me."

"Is anything I wrote not true?"

"I mean . . . you don't understand," I stammer. "First of all, how did you even find out about all this stuff?"

Brooke crosses her arms. "I'll never reveal my sources!"

"Brooke," I growl.

"Fine. A few weeks ago, Tristen was working on a puff piece

about style trends among teachers. She googled Mr. Kimbrough to try to find some pictures of him and came across Humble Pi. She sent it to me and I started doing some digging."

"Tristen?" This is not computing.

"I saw the Galgorithm post on the blog," she continues, "and it immediately looked familiar. I recognized some of those tricks from when Anthony and I first started going out. I confronted him about it, and he caved pretty quickly."

Goddamn it, Hedgehog.

"He told me all about your little scheme."

"It's not a scheme!"

She ignores me.

"I looked through all of your Facebook friends and noticed that you had a few random older friends."

Somehow I've always known that Mark Zuckerberg would screw me.

"I also noticed that some of those friends had one thing in common: They were dating girls way out of their league."

No such thing!

I keep my mouth shut.

"I put two and two together," she continues, "and reached out to them. A few of them were former clients who had already graduated. They agreed to talk to me if I kept them anonymous."

So cold. Sold out by my own clients.

"And you didn't think to come to me to get my side before you printed anything?"

"I knew you would have just freaked out and denied everything and had Mr. Kimbrough take it down."

"Damn right I would have freaked out!"

"Exactly."

"Oh, so you have your little scoop and that's all that matters?" I say. "I thought we were friends. Well, congratulations, this is much bigger than Watermelongate."

"If fruit salad is advertised on the menu, it should include watermelon! Our tax dollars pay for that food!"

I try to get back to the point.

"Brooke, you don't understand. There's no such thing as the Galgorithm. That thing on Mr. Kimbrough's blog, I've never seen it before in my life. He created it on his own. There was no Galgorithm until he made one!"

"So all those pickup lines and little tricks, those aren't yours?" She arches an eyebrow.

"No. I mean, yes. I mean, they used to be. It's complicated."

"Try me."

"That thing on the blog, it makes it seem like there is some algorithm to get girls. There's not. You can't distill everything they do down to a number. That's not how it works. The whole thing needs a human touch. Someone to interpret everything."

"So that's what you do? You're an interpreter for guys who you label nerds? Like some kind of dork whisperer?"

I don't even know where to begin. "Brooke, this isn't even me anymore. I'm retired. Out of the game."

This does not satisfy her in the slightest.

"I just want to make sure I'm clear. So you never advised your clients to use the same technique as Pavlov's dogs?"

I sigh. "Yes and no."

"Go on."

"*Obviously* Pavlovian conditioning doesn't work on human girls."

Just saying these words makes me feel like such a tool. Brooke rolls her eyes. I need to explain.

"I mean, the reason I advise—*advised*—my clients to be near the girl they like when the girl gets good news is *not* so that the girl will somehow eventually associate good news with the guy."

"Then what's the reason?"

"It's to help the guy start to feel comfortable around the girl. It's to give him a specific time and place every day or every week when all he's thinking about is the girl. It's to give the guy a moment to look forward to when he knows the girl he is pining after will be all smiles and good vibrations. It's to give him hope."

"Uh huh," Brooke says, unconvinced. "Yeah, well, I didn't really appreciate finding out that Anthony was stalking me for months before we went out."

"He wasn't stalking you! I was there. He was *learning* about you so that he could have a meaningful conversation with you once he got up the nerve to even talk to you. Anthony will tell you himself. Where is he?"

"I don't know. We broke up."

No.

"What do you mean you broke up?"

"I mean, when I found out what he did, and I put all the pieces together, I ended it. Just before we went to press."

"What he *did*? He adored you. He was devoted to you. Years before you even knew he existed."

"I know. And that's weird."

"But you can't break up. You're Hedgehog and Balloon. You're the perfect couple. You're *totes adorbs*."

"We're not Hedgehog and Balloon anymore."

"Okay, time-out: I understand why Anthony is Hedgehog, but why are you called Balloon?"

She loudly *CLAPS* her hands in front of my face, startling me.

"Because I *pop* when you least expect it."

"Jesus Christ. Really?"

"No, it's because when I laugh it sounds really squeaky, like a balloon."

"Oh."

"You messed up, Shane. You lied to a lot of people. And a lot of people are hurt."

My mind suddenly starts to wander. . . .

"Shane," she continues, "are you listening to me? Shane?"

I need to find Jak.

35

JAK HAS VANISHED. She didn't respond to any of my calls or texts. She wasn't at her locker at any of her usual times. She didn't even go to any of her afternoon classes—including Ms. Solomon's history class, which I barged into only to find Jak's seat in the back row unoccupied. I checked all our usual haunts. She wasn't in the cafeteria or the courtyard. I called her house, and her mom said she hadn't come home from school yet. I even drove to Perkin's Beanery to see if she was hiding out there. No dice.

It's a million-to-one shot, but I decide to look one more place and blow right past Zoey with a *y* or Sofia with an *f* or whoever is currently manning the front desk at Sweat Republic. I search the gym floor and the treadmills, but Jak's not there. Finally I check the yoga studio in the back. It has clear glass windows, but the lights are off. I walk inside and flick the lights on, and that's where I find her: sitting on an oversize ab ball in the corner, staring at the wall. It would be a depressing sight if she didn't look so beautiful.

"Jak!"

She doesn't respond. I cross the hardwood floor, grab another ab ball, and sit on it next to her. She's furious and doesn't acknowledge me.

"I've been looking all over for you. Are you okay?" She doesn't answer. I'm not sure what to do. "I guess neither of us is having a sweat-tastic day," I offer.

She rotates away from me on her ball. My attempt at lightening the mood has fallen flat.

"Jak, the whole thing in the paper is totally blown out of proportion. Is that what you're upset about? Because I don't do that stuff anymore. The whole Galgorithm thing is made up."

She rotates back so that we are side by side but she doesn't have to look at me.

"I thought I knew you," she says.

"You *do* know me, Jak. You do know me. You knew I helped some of the nerdy guys talk to girls."

"I thought you were just messing around. I thought it was just for fun. Shane, I didn't know the extent. I didn't know that you had half the school on your roster."

"Come on, Jak. I didn't have half the school on my roster."

"And that *formula*?"

"It's not real, Jak. Mr. Kimbrough created it. The Galgorithm was just a silly name I made up for my services. The whole thing is silly."

"Your *services?*"

I realize this is having the opposite of the intended effect and making me sound even *more* creepy.

"Not services. My . . . assistance."

"It couldn't have been *that* silly a thing, Shane. You kept it a secret from me."

She's got me there.

"Jak . . ."

"I thought we told each other everything."

"We do. It was just this one dumb thing that I didn't even think was *worth* telling you. I had *one* secret. Sue me."

I contemplate *why* I didn't tell Jak about everything in the first place, years ago. I wonder if, just maybe, these feelings I have for her now have been there all along. Maybe a part of me has always been in love with Jak. Maybe *that's* why I didn't want her to judge me for what I was doing.

"He used it on me," she murmurs.

"Huh?"

"That thing. The Galgorithm. Adam used some of that stuff on me. He's one of your clients, isn't he?"

I hesitate.

"Was. Yeah. I guess that's another thing I should have told you."

"So you tricked him into liking me?"

"No! Not at all! He liked you all on his own. In fact, he didn't even *tell me* that he was interested in you. I actually kinda got mad that he went behind my back to talk to you. He did it by himself."

"But he used the stuff *you* taught him."

"Jak, it doesn't really work like that. Every case is different."

"Case."

"I don't mean it like that. I mean just because Adam used to be a client doesn't mean I taught him how to hit on you."

That doesn't sound much better.

"But then all of a sudden he was over me and into Rebecca. Was that you too?"

"No! I mean . . . not technically."

"Why, Shane? Why did you get involved?"

This is not the moment to tell her how I feel. Not here. Not like this. I can't drop a bombshell like that on her now. It's not fair. It will feel like an excuse. It will put all the pressure on her.

"Why, Shane?" she repeats.

I shrug. I feel awful. I never should have gotten involved in Jak's dating life, no matter what I was thinking at the time.

"I thought I did something dumb at the party," she says. "I thought that was why Adam didn't like me anymore."

Jak is more upset about Adam than she was letting on. But mostly, I can tell, she's disappointed in me.

She rotates away from me again. She's crying. I have not seen Jak cry since we were little kids. It's heartbreaking.

"Please don't cry."

"Am I not enough for you?" she asks.

"What do you mean?"

"Am I not enough for you? Is your life so empty that you need to fill it with other people's problems? You've been MIA for months. Why do you think I got the Fitbits and the gym membership? So you would actually hang out with me. But this is how you've been spending your time? I counted on you. Do you know how much that hurts?"

"Jak, all of this is behind me. The clients, the cases, the formula. I gave it up."

"Well, it's not behind me. I . . . I don't know. I thought we had something special."

"We *do* have something special."

She starts to sob. She shakes her head. "No. Not anymore. You've changed. You're different now."

"I'm not, Jak. I'm still the same. It's me, Shane the Mane. Please stop crying."

She wipes her nose on the sleeve of her shirt like a little kid. So damn endearing.

"You're not the same. I liked the old Shane. I liked baggy-jeans Shane. Pocket-protector Shane. That Shane was all right."

"I'm still that Shane!"

"That Shane wasn't too busy for me. That Shane didn't backstab me. That Shane was my best friend."

I get off my ab ball and get down on one knee in front of Jak so she is forced to look at me.

"Please, Jak. Don't do this."

"*I* didn't do anything, Shane. *You* did this."

"We can work this out. We always do. We can still be besties."

"We can't," she says. "You lied to me. You kept secrets from me. You betrayed me."

"One day we'll look back at this and laugh."

"Maybe *you* will," she says as she stands up.

I'm still on my knee on the floor. She takes her Fitbit off and gives it to me. I feel like she is handing me her bloodied heart on a platter.

"Don't talk to me anymore. Don't call me. Don't text me. I don't want to know you."

"Please," I say. "Jak, let me make it up to you. I can make this right."

"I thought I was different," she says. "I thought you treated me better."

"You are! I do!"

"Yeah, well, I hope your next best friend is more understanding."

And with that she walks out of the room, but not before shutting off the lights and leaving me in the dark.

36

THE PAST WEEK OR SO has been a blur. And not the good kind of blur, either. A really, really bad blur. Devastated by the Galgorithm exposé and my falling out with Jak, I've tried to avoid my other classmates as much as possible. Fortunately, AP exams were administered at the middle school in Kingsview, which kept me away from much of the high school population for a few days. On the other days, I stayed home, either claiming to be studying or faking sick.

I think my exams went fine. I felt strangely in the zone during the tests because it was a bit of relief from the chaos in my personal life. Who knew that humiliation and heartbreak could be a substitute for Adderall.

Meanwhile, the baseball team has begun its playoff push, led by my archnemesis Harrison. I have stayed far away from the games, of course. I don't really care about baseball anyway, but am secretly rooting for us to maintain this winning streak. It keeps Harrison focused more on charging the batter's box at the tiniest provocation and less on charging at me.

We've reached mid-May and there's only six weeks of high school left, but I feel totally numb. Being without Jak has been the hardest part. She's completely shut me out. Won't return my texts. Blocked me on Insta. Something that has been a part of me my whole life is now suddenly gone; I feel like I'm missing a limb. I've tried to apologize to her every way I know how, but nothing seems sufficient.

My feelings for Jak have not diminished or wavered in any way. If anything, they've only intensified. I love her and I want to spend every waking moment we have left together, which makes our rift that much more painful. She's totally disappeared from my world. If absence makes the heart grow fonder, then my heart has grown as fond as possible and is about to burst out of my chest.

I've tried to tell Tristen that she should move on, that I'm not the right guy for her, and that she deserves better. But as much as Jak refuses to let me in, Tristen refuses to let me go.

I feel like I've been misunderstood. Not just by Jak, but by everyone who read the article about me and gasped. People seem to think that I was pulling strings and scheming behind the scenes. But all my advice ever did was stop guys from being their own worst enemies.

Right now, though, I'm learning that the benefits of all my advice are only temporary. When I spot Reed sitting in a booth at the pizza place on Hickory—the site of his and Marisol's first date—I immediately notice a difference in him. His posture is poor. His hair is unkempt. His T-shirt is rumpled. I'm pretty sure he's wearing those dumpy jeans his mom bought him. Probably no belt, either. In the time since the Galgorithm was exposed, Reed has regressed to his old self. His swagger is gone.

I join him in the booth. "Hey, man."

"Hey, Shane," he says, not as enthusiastically as the last time we chatted, but friendly nonetheless.

"Thanks for suggesting this," I say. "I really needed to get out of the house."

"No problem," he says. "I have a lot of good memories of this place."

The restaurant is small, only a few tables, and there's no air-conditioning, just two ceiling fans. It's hot, and the walls are red brick, so it feels like you're actually *inside* a brick pizza oven.

Reed hasn't ordered yet, so I figure I'll just wait until he's ready. In the meantime, there are some unfortunate developments that need to be discussed.

"I heard about Marisol," I say.

Reed hangs his head.

Like Brooke, when Marisol saw the article and blog post

about the Galgorithm, she thought some of the "techniques" seemed familiar. Eventually she figured out that Reed was a client of mine. Then she broke up with him.

"It sucks, Shane."

"Remember how one of the very first things I ever taught you was to be positive as much as possible and to apologize as little as possible?"

"Yeah," he says.

"I think it's okay to be negative now. And also: *I'm sorry.*"

Something makes me think I'm gonna be apologizing a lot in the coming weeks.

"Hey, if it wasn't for you, I never would have been dating Marisol in the first place."

"Still, if she broke up with you over something I did, then it's my fault. What did she say?"

"Just that she was embarrassed. And she felt like I lied to her. Like our whole relationship was based on me being creepy."

"Have you tried talking to her since? Given her some time to cool off?"

"Right now she's not returning any of my calls." He sighs. "I figure if I can't be with Marisol, then I don't want to be with anyone else. So I changed back to my old clothes. That way no one will ever want to date me, like it's supposed to be."

"Don't say that, Reed. You know as well as I do that Marisol never went for you because you updated your wardrobe."

"Is this where you give me the 'it's what's inside that counts' speech? Because I'm really not in the mood."

"Fair enough," I say, allowing him space. "So what's the scene been like at school?"

"Oh, you know Kingsview. Everyone's got the attention span of a fruit fly. A lot of people have moved on. The baseball team is all the rage now. Some of the girls are still pissed. But you've developed quite the cult following among the, let's say, socially challenged crowd."

This I knew. Every nerd, geek, and dweeb in town has been messaging me asking for advice. *Advice for what?* I think to myself. How to end up alone? I haven't responded to any of them.

"Have you seen Jak?" I ask.

"She's around. Kinda has a sour look on her face."

"Hmm. That doesn't really mean anything. That's her normal look. She looks that way on her birthday."

Reed shrugs.

"Let me ask you a question," I say. "Me and Jak. When you were around us, did you ever think that, I don't know, maybe we could be more than just friends?"

He chuckles.

"What?" I ask.

"Are you kidding me? You two are like obsessed with each other. I've never seen two 'friends' who more obviously want to hook up."

"Are you serious?"

"Yes! I mean, clearly you're in love with her. Me and a couple of my Dungeons and Dragons buddies used to make fun of you on Twitter. 'Shane and Jak equals #Shak.'"

"A hashtag? Really?"

"Hey, before you took me on as a client, I had a lot of free time."

"How come you never told me that I was in love with her!"

"It's kind of a thing you gotta figure out on your own."

Very, very true. Though running into Faith also didn't hurt. Either way, it doesn't matter. I ruined everything with Jak.

Reed and I stare into space for a while, each pondering our meager existence. I used to think that Reed could be my protégé. Then he swept Marisol off her feet, and I thought the pupil had become the master. Now I look at us as equals: two hopeless outcasts.

This can't be how it ends.

"Reed, you know what would be even sweeter than winning over Marisol in the first place?" I ask.

"Being a male model who women flock to without even trying?"

"Well, yeah, I guess that would be pretty sweet. But what I was gonna say was winning her back."

"Winning Marisol back?"

"Yeah!" I say, trying to pump Reed up.

"I don't know. I think I might need to take a break."

"I'm telling you, you could do it, Reed. You don't even need me anymore. I already taught you everything I know."

"You really believe that?"

I can tell his confidence is buried in there, somewhere.

"Absolutely," I say. "But this time, you do it on your terms. Don't be embarrassed about playing Dungeons and Dragons. Don't hide that from her. Don't spend hours planning and preparing. Just do it. Just like you did that day in the courtyard. That should be your whole relationship: going with your gut, being yourself, owning you!"

Reed starts to nod his head. As far as motivational speeches go, this hasn't been my finest. But I just want Reed to know that he can do it.

"Okay," he says. "Maybe you're right. If me and Marisol were meant to be together, then we should be together, no matter what."

"Exactly!"

"I'm just gonna talk to her, I'm gonna be honest, I'm gonna explain myself, I'm gonna apologize, and then she's gonna take me back!"

"That's the spirit."

It's the first time in a while that either of us has smiled.

"Huzzah!" I shout, and Reed beams.

37

I FINALLY GET THE COURAGE to suck it up and head back to school with my head held high.

Okay, that's not really true. I'm only going to school after trying to push my luck and fake sick for one more day. My parents called my bluff. Next thing I knew I was in my Jeep, driving into the eye of the storm.

After I park, I walk the most circuitous route possible from my car to the school. I'm still trying to steel myself to face my peers and possibly—hopefully—run into Jak. I make the ill-fated decision to cut through the faculty lot, and it is there that I see the source of much of my troubles: Mr. Kimbrough, slumped in his car once again, moping.

Apparently, my pity for the guy knows no bounds, or

maybe I'm just procrastinating, because I decide to make my way to his car. He doesn't even notice as I walk up to the driver's-side window.

"Let me guess," I say. "Deb ended things."

He doesn't look at me or say anything but acknowledges I'm correct by solemnly unlocking the passenger side door. Mr. Kimbrough could rightly be blamed for destroying my life. But for some reason I have a soft spot for him. I can't hold a grudge. He deserves to be as happy as the next guy. And I sure as hell don't want to end up like him when I'm in my thirties. I reluctantly get in the car.

"What happened?" I ask.

He takes a deep breath. "Well, thanks to you, Deb finally started responding to my texts. She eventually told me that she had feelings for me, and that she only went radio silent after we spent the night together because it freaked her out that we're coworkers."

"Ahhh," I say. At least that's one mystery solved.

"And then we started chatting again," he continues. "We had lunch one day. I thought we were hitting it off. We had plans to go out."

"So, what? She found out about the Galgorithm, got offended, and that was that?"

"Basically, yeah."

"Stupid school newspaper. I mean, who even reads that thing anyway? Instead of running editorials about how we need two-ply toilet paper in the bathrooms, how about using the *Chronicle* to wipe your—"

"Shane," Mr. Kimbrough interjects. "You don't understand. Deb didn't find out about the Galgorithm from the newspaper."

"Yeah, well, people were talking about it in the halls, it was all over Facebook . . ."

"No, I mean Deb knew about the Galgorithm *before* it was in the paper."

"How is that possible?"

"She read my blog, Shane."

"Okay . . ."

"No, I mean I never told her about Humble Pi. In fact, I kept it a secret from her. After we reconnected and we had lunch, she must have found the blog herself and started reading it *on her own*. She liked my blog, Shane! *My* blog! She liked *me*! And I screwed it up."

He buries his face in his hands.

"I'm sorry, Bob." I pat him on the shoulder. "But I still don't understand what you were thinking. I mean, if what I was telling you was working so well, why post it for everyone to see? Why risk Deb *ever* knowing?"

He looks at me. "I don't know! I was just so excited. I wasn't thinking straight. I didn't think anyone would care. No one ever went to my blog. I certainly didn't think Deb had it bookmarked."

I shake my head. Love will make you do crazy things.

"After I saw you in the computer lab," he continues, "I tried to head her off. But it was already too late. She told me that she'd read that post the day before. She also told me she was disgusted and that she never wanted to speak to me again. I tried to tell her it was meant to be a joke. But she wouldn't have any of it. Not after I used it on her."

I feel bad for Bob. I was growing to like Ms. Solomon. I mean, she single-handedly rescued me from Harrison in the student-government office. And she didn't bat an eye when I interrupted her class while searching for Jak. She's good people.

"Again, Shane, I'm really sorry for all the trouble I caused you. You went out of your way to help me, a pathetic old teacher, and I repaid you by totally botching everything. I took advantage of your trust, and I'm really embarrassed by my behavior."

"It's okay. Things happen." I sorta believe what I'm saying.

"Well, if it makes you feel any better," he says, "I decided to take the entire blog down after all. Who knows how far it's already spread, but at this point I'd rather just be done with it. Also I didn't want to get fired. I'm on thin ice as it is."

"Huh," I say. "So the Galgorithm and Humble Pi are both retired. It's truly the end of an era."

"Yeah, I was sad to hear you'll no longer be . . . advising

the less fortunate," Mr. Kimbrough says. "That seems like the kind of thing that would serve you well in college."

"Nah," I say. "That's not who I am anymore. It's too much of a crutch. Something to hide behind. I need to start taking my own advice and just be me."

As soon as I figure out who that is. . . .

"So what about Deb?" I ask.

"I don't know," Bob says. "I miss her. I miss just hearing her voice."

"Is it worth it for you to try to talk to her again and explain?" I ask.

"I don't think so. I mean, we work together. It was probably inappropriate for me to ask her out in the first place. Plus she just got direct deposit. So there go all those Thursdays when I got to stand next to her while she tore open those checks. She was always so happy. I really looked forward to those days."

"Out of curiosity, did you—"

"Notice any Pavlovian conditioning? No. Not at all. But I did enjoy getting to spend that time with her."

"Got it. Thought so."

"Seeing her around school lately has been tough. Knowing I hurt her. Knowing I had a chance but I ruined it. I realize it sounds corny and we didn't date that long . . . but I think I was falling for her."

"Hey, Bob. Never say never."

"I just wish I hadn't acted like the square root of two."

I shake my head. "What?"

"Irrational. I wish I hadn't been so irrational."

I pat Bob on the shoulder again. I'm surprisingly glad he hasn't lost his sense of humor.

38

I **WAIT UNTIL MR. KIMBROUGH** has gathered himself, and then we get out of his car together. When he's finally ready to head into school, though, I leave him to double back to grab my phone, which I forgot in my own car.

When I get close to my parking spot, I see a magnificent sight: Tristen, with her back to me, bent over next to my car, in those short jean shorts I love so much. But my initial arousal very quickly turns to dismay—*what the hell is she doing?*

I jog the last twenty feet to my car, calling her name. She quickly stands up and coyly hides something behind her back. I immediately expect the worst.

"Tristen," I say when I reach her, "please don't tell me you're slashing my tires or something crazy like that."

She shakes her head no.

"Then what are you doing?"

She shows me her hands: She's holding a pen and a piece of paper.

"I was leaving you a note. Your tire is low."

Now I feel bad.

"Oh. Um, thanks."

Then I hear the *sssssssssssss* of air leaking from my front right tire, right where Tristen is standing. I take a closer look. The valve has been loosened.

"Were you leaving me a note . . . *after* you let the air out?"

She shrugs.

My relationship with Tristen has been a roller coaster. First I underestimated her. Then we totally connected. Unfortunately, that coincided with me starting to crush on Jak. I've been trying to end things with Tristen, but instead have fallen into a trap as old as time: By pushing her away, I've unintentionally made her like me even more. Most disconcerting is how erratic Tristen has been behaving lately, for instance right now.

"You're back at school!" she says, as my tire continues to leak. "Are you feeling better?"

I recall that Tristen is the one who first discovered Humble Pi and showed it to Brooke. Which means Tristen could have known for weeks that I used the Galgorithm on her. Maybe she's just upset and this is her way of acting out.

"Listen," I say, "I know you're mad. And I *totally* get it."

"I'm not mad."

"You're not?"

"No!"

"Then why are you letting the air out of my tire?"

"Duh. I want attention."

I have to hand it to her. At least she's stone-cold honest.

"But you saw the article in the *Chronicle* right? You know what I used to do? You know about the Galgorithm?"

"Of course. I know all about it."

"And that makes you feel . . ."

"Super turned on."

"Turned *on*?"

"Totally. I mean, how cute are you to help all those lonely guys? Like, who does that? Plus you know all these things about women. Like, stuff we never tell anybody. That's so hot."

"You do realize that everyone else is mad at me, right? Marisol broke up with Reed over it."

"Oh, she's just being silly," she says dismissively.

"You don't care that I used all that stuff on you?"

"I wish you would do it more. That's why I didn't say anything even though I knew the article was coming out."

"Tristen, you could have warned me!"

"Shane, I *like* the Galgorithm."

Wait a minute, I think. *The Galgorithm!* Maybe that's the way to resist Tristen. Maybe I take all my old tips, and do them in reverse. Yeah, that could work! What's the opposite of "be different, notice her, tell her"? Be the same, ignore her, don't tell her? That doesn't make any sense! What's the opposite of "be positive, never apologize"? Be negative . . . always apologize? What? No. Oh my God. What am I doing? I've gone completely insane.

"Shane," she continues, "do you remember how I was raising money for dolphins in the Congo?"

"Huh? Yeah, of course."

"Well, this summer, after my Habitat for Humanity trip, I think I'm gonna travel there to actually *see* the dolphins. I want you to come with me. It'll be totes amaze."

"Me and you, alone, in the Congo?"

"Well, technically Gabon, but yes."

"Um . . ."

"Just think about it."

It's time to put my foot down.

"I'm sorry, Tristen, but no. This is over."

"Whatever you say . . ."

"I'm serious. We can't be together."

"Will you unlock your car, please?"

"Why?" I'm so confused.

"Just unlock it."

"Argh." I foolishly click my keychain and unlock the doors. Tristen smirks, then opens the back door, grabs me by my shirt, and pushes me into the car. For someone with such spindly forearms, she's surprisingly aggro. Before I even know what's happening, she's straddling me in the backseat.

"Tristen, wait."

"No more talking." She starts kissing me. Keep in mind it's seven forty-five in the morning.

"Tristen, there are people around."

"I don't care."

I can't believe Tristen is behaving like this. She was so normal for so long. And she could have any guy she wanted!

She kisses my neck and nibbles on my earlobe. She knows that's my spot.

"Tristen . . ." My resolve is crumbling. I hate how weak I am.

But, I rationalize, I also deserve someone who wants me. I deserve this.

I kiss Tristen back. I pull her closer. She starts to moan.

I'm only human.

I run my hands along her back and her sides. She moans some more.

"Hooooo. Hooooo."

It's kind of a strange moan. I disregard it and kiss her neck. She moans again.

"Hooooo. Hooooo."

She sounds like an owl. I don't care. This is happening.

"Hooooo. Hooooo."

And that's when I realize she's not moaning "Hooooo," she's saying "Whooooom," as in "whom."

"Whooooom. Whooooom."

I stop caressing her. I stop kissing her.

"Are you saying 'whom'?"

She starts to grind on me. "Yeah," she says breathlessly. "Whooooom."

I grab her shoulders.

"Why? Why are you saying that?"

"I know it's important to you. *I* want to be important to you too."

I take my hands off her.

This isn't right. For so many reasons.

Jak would never pull a stunt like this. Jak would never have to try this hard. Even if she won't speak to me right now, Jak is the only girl for me. I cannot continue to let Tristen distract me from that. Tristen is fun. But Jak is the One.

"Whooooom," she repeats.

39

THIS TREE HAS A LOT of history. It emerges from the ground right at the corner where Jak and I go our separate ways when we walk home from school together. The middle school in Kingsview is only a few blocks from the high school, so we walked the same route past this tree for six years before we got our licenses, and then the tradition resumed when Jak got us Fitbits. On many of those walks, Jak has playfully tried to push me into this very tree. It's gnarled and knotty and has a bunch of hearts carved into it by lovers or pranksters or both.

After managing to extricate myself from Tristen's clutches, which took a lot of negotiating and a few whistles from some passing freshmen, I didn't even bother going to class. I had too much on my mind. I just left my car in the lot, still leaking air, and have been walking the route from school to my house over and over again, for hours. By now, though, school has ended. I'm waiting by the tree for Jak to drive past in the hopes of flagging her down and begging her forgiveness.

I must repair my friendship with Jak. That's the most important thing in the world to me. But, should I get the chance, I also need to tell her how I truly feel. This may not be the perfect moment, but there may never be a perfect moment. I can't keep it inside any longer.

I spot Jak down the block, driving her dark gray Prius, and step out into the street. As she gets closer, I get cold feet. I want to run. But something keeps me in place, rooted to the ground, just like the tree.

Now Jak is close enough to recognize me, but I can't really see her reaction inside the car. I wave my arms. She could easily drive around me, or she could stop. Relief washes over me when I hear the electronic *whooosh* of the Prius decelerating. She pulls over and stops on the side of the road in front of me.

She gets out of the car and approaches, scowling.

"What are you doing?"

"I need to talk to you," I say.

"How long have you been out here?"

"All day."

"You're an idiot."

"I know. That's what I wanted to talk to you about. Will you give me a minute?"

She glances at her wrist and sighs overdramatically. She's not even wearing a watch. "Ugh. One minute."

I take a deep breath. "Jak. I'm sorry I lied to you. I'm sorry I kept secrets from you. I'm sorry I hurt you. I really, truly am. Everything I did I did with good intentions. You know that. You know me."

Her face doesn't change.

"Words."

"Words are all I've got right now, Jak. But I swear to God, I will do whatever it takes, for as long as it takes, to make it up to you."

"If this whole Galgorithm thing was such a big part of your life," she asks, "then why did you keep it from me?"

"I don't know."

"Why didn't you tell me everything that you were really doing? Why did you have to have this stupid alter ego I didn't know about?"

"Everything just spiraled out of control. I should have told you."

"That's not good enough, Shane. That doesn't make any sense. That's so dumb."

"You're right."

"I want to know what happened with Adam."

I suddenly can't find the words.

"What did you do?" she asks.

"Umm," I mumble.

Why am I so eloquent in my head!

A car zooms by and momentarily distracts us.

Jak resumes her focus on me.

"Who the hell do you think you are?"

"Jak, I can explain."

I tread carefully, knowing that whatever I say next I cannot unsay. Once this is out of the bag, nothing will ever be the same.

"Why did you hurt me like that, Shane?"

"Because I love you."

I have to catch my breath. I said it. I did it.

Jak looks more confused than anything.

"What?"

"I love you," I repeat. "I told Adam I had feelings for you, and that's why he got weird. The truth is I love you. I'm *in* love with you, Jak."

"Like . . . you *love me* love me?"

"Yes."

"Is this a joke?"

This is not as romantic as I envisioned it.

"No! It's not a joke. I love everything about you. Your legs, your brain, your eyelashes with the split ends. Everything. That's why I got involved between you and Adam."

Jak doesn't say anything. I take some solace in the fact that her expression has morphed from angry to befuddled. It's a start, I guess.

"Where is this coming from?" she asks finally.

"I don't know, Jak. Where does it ever come from? All I know is that I love you and that's why I did the stupid things I did."

"How long have you felt this way?"

"When we were in the bathtub together, after the party. That's when I first started to know. But a part of me thinks it was always there. Maybe even from the beginning. From the first bathtub."

"No," she says.

"No what?"

"No you're not *allowed* to be in love with me, Shane. We're best friends."

"I can't help what I feel, Jak. The question is, do you feel the same way? Because I think you do."

I'm looking for any change in her eyes, her breathing, anything.

"Shane, after what we just went through, how could you possibly ask me something like that? Our friendship is hanging by a thread."

"I need to know."

"I told you, years ago, after Voldemort, that we could never be together. You were a train wreck. I can't go through that with you."

I shake my head. "I never got to tell you," I say. "I saw Voldemort that day I found you hiding out in the gym. The day everything went down. . . ."

"You did?"

"Yeah. At the mall. Even she thinks we should be together."

"Why should I care what that skank thinks?"

Though it's not helping my argument right now, it does warm my heart to know that Jak is still defending my honor after all these years.

"Even the kids at school think we should be together," I say. "They call us #Shak."

"Shane, I don't care what other people think."

The phrase "I don't care what other people think" gets thrown around a lot. But Jak actually means it. She walks the walk. It's another thing that, although it's working against me now, I truly admire about her.

"Jak, you never answered my question. *Do you feel the same way?*"

"No," she says, finally. "I don't."

She looks down at the ground so that she doesn't have to face me.

It can't be. Pressure builds in my sinuses and I feel like my head is gonna implode.

"You just don't want me to be mad at you anymore," she says. "That's all this is."

"That's not true!"

I'm still trying to search Jak's face for any clue that she might be holding back. But she has no tell. I'm starting to feel nauseous.

"Well," I manage, "*are* you still mad at me?"

She shrugs.

"Jak, you said you thought we had something special. We *do* have something special. It's just more special than friendship. It's even better."

"We're going away to college in a few months."

"I know," I say. "And why do you think we like never talk about that?"

"You're with Tristen."

"It's over."

No reaction.

"You can come up with a million reasons why we shouldn't be together, Jak. But there's only one reason why we *should*: We love each other."

"I don't know what you want me to say, Shane."

"Tell me you love me too."

She shakes her head no. Is she telling me no? Or is she trying to convince herself?

She looks away once more.

"I don't. Not in that way," she says.

I stare at her. Try to make sense of what's going on in that big brain of hers. It's the worst possible outcome for me, but I think she's telling the truth.

I'm devastated. I feel sick. I sit down on the curb and hang my head between my knees. I can see Jak's white Chucks shuffling in the street in front of me.

After a moment she sits next to me on the curb.

After another moment she asks, "Are you okay?"

Her voice is steady. Her tone is concerned. She might even still be a little annoyed with me. But she's not mad.

"No, I'm not okay," I say. "I'm in love with you. Don't you understand that? I'm opening up to you."

I'm distraught. I knew this was a risk. But bracing for it doesn't change how terrible this is.

"I'm sorry, Shane. I can't change how I feel. Besides, this is exactly what I was worried about. One of us getting hurt. And things getting weird."

"I promise that won't happen," I say, to no avail.

I'm trying not to hyperventilate.

"I would be disappointed if I were you too," Jak says. "I'm the bomb."

This finally manages to elicit an involuntary grin out of me.

I look at her. My feelings haven't changed. I still want her more than anything. Maybe I don't blame her for rejecting me. Maybe I'm just glad she's talking to me again. If she hasn't forgiven me outright, she's at least softened her stance. And I have to be grateful for that. If and how we move forward from here, though, is anyone's guess.

"Come on, Incredible Sulk," she says. "I'll give you a ride home."

She stands up, using my shoulder for balance. Her touch sends shivers down my extremities.

She walks over to her car, then stops and turns to me.

There are three little words that I'm praying for her to utter.

"Are you coming?"

Those aren't them.

Jak is soldiering on. I can't believe this is happening.

I rise from the curb unsteadily and start to walk to the car, but not before glancing at all the hearts on the tree on the corner, and trying to accept that Jak and I will never share one.

40

I WAS A REALLY CUTE little kid. Jak, not so much.

I'm sitting at the kitchen table with my laptop, staring at a scanned version of the picture of me and Jak in the bathtub as babies. I'm freakin' adorable. Jak's nose is scrunched up and her face is already sour like she hates the world. I smile every time I look at the picture. But now there is an undercurrent of sadness. It reminds me that this is as far as our relationship will ever go.

I search for #Shak on Twitter. There are a lot of posts about Shakira. Those hips don't lie. But if I scroll back far enough, I find a handful of tweets from Reed and his friends that reference me and Jak. Most of them are in the vein of "get a room." But taken together they paint a poignant picture of how outsiders view us: essentially, star-crossed lovers in total denial. Some are from years ago. I kick myself for being so blind. But I also realize that without Jak as a willing participant, the whole thing is futile anyway.

My one saving grace is that Jak is no longer giving me the cold shoulder. Our friendship is far from mended—she's still peeved at my duplicity, and my proclamation of love has not served to make things any less awkward—but at least we're communicating again. I wish that fact would do more to mitigate the excruciating pain I feel about getting rejected by her. What is the lesson I'm supposed to take away from all this? That when you finally let down your guard, shed your armor, and put yourself out there, you get screwed six ways to Sunday? I don't imagine you'll ever see that on a motivational poster of a kitten.

I stare blankly at my computer screen for a while, letting my mind wander into dark and depressing places, but snap out of it when I hear my parents arguing in the living room downstairs. They get into tiffs here and there, but they're not loud and vociferous like some of the other parents I've witnessed, so it's kind of disconcerting to hear them go at it.

Mom and Dad are on Facebook, so eventually they found out about the Galgorithm scandal. But I stridently downplayed it and was able to convince them that it wasn't that big a deal. Parents never want to believe that their kids are ever in any real trouble, and so I fed them the narrative that the whole escapade was just a bad joke gone too far, and that it had blown over (which at least has a morsel of truthiness to it). I haven't told them anything about the situation with Jak.

I hear even louder shouting coming from downstairs, and now I'm starting to get a little nervous. Maybe the tenor of their arguments *has* been getting a bit more vitriolic over the past few months. What's gonna happen when I go away to college and I'm not here to keep an eye on things? I'm still not over the fact that Hedgehog and Balloon are finished. If there is even a hint of a crack in my parents' marriage, I'm just gonna give up.

I wander downstairs to discover that the shouting isn't coming from the living room, but the basement, which is one floor below that. I find my parents on their hands and knees, digging through a storage closet in the back of the room.

"Peter, I'm telling you, it's not in that box. I already looked in that box!"

"Did you *really* look, though?" my dad responds. "'Cause I'm ninety-nine percent sure that's where it is."

"Yes, I'm sure, and I don't appreciate that tone."

"Well, we've been at this for twenty minutes now, Kathryn, so I really don't know what kind of tone you expect!"

"Guys!" I interject. "What's going on?"

Mom pulls her head out from the closet.

"Oh, hi, honey!" she says.

She actually doesn't seem to be that upset at all.

"Dad and I were feeling a bit nostalgic, so we're looking for that album we recorded together in college."

"Found it!" Dad says, emerging from the closet triumphantly clutching a CD.

"And was it in the box that I already looked in?" Mom asks.

"Nope," Dad says sheepishly. "You were right. I was wrong. Don't get too used to hearing me say that."

They smile at each other. All is not lost.

My dad also digs out an old stereo with a CD player. We set it up on top of a nearby dresser and pop in the album.

I hear a beautiful voice singing an a cappella rendition of "Motownphilly" by Boyz II Men. I've heard my mom hum around the house before, but never anything like this.

"Mom, that's *you*?"

"There were a lot of talented gals in that a cappella group," Dad says, "but your mom was the best. I remember that day like it was yesterday."

"It didn't hurt to have you staring at me from the sound booth."

They make googly eyes at each other.

"But even after all that, it still took you guys five years to get together?" I ask.

"True love takes time," Dad says.

This gives me no comfort.

Mom pauses the CD. "You sure everything is all right, honey? You've been moping around for weeks now."

"Yeah," I say. "It's just that . . ."

Should I say something? I don't know. It's so embarrassing talking to my parents.

"Girl stuff or whatever," I mutter. "I just wish I understood what they were thinking." That's about as much detail as I can bear to provide.

My parents give each other a knowing look.

"I've known your mother for more than two decades," Dad says. "And I still have no clue what she's thinking. I have no idea what she's thinking right now."

"It's true," Mom chimes in.

"Besides," Dad continues, "why would you *want* to understand women? That's half the fun. I love that your mother is so inscrutable."

Mom and Dad kiss.

"Avocados, by the way," Mom says.

"What?" Dad says.

"That's what I was thinking about. I need to buy avocados."

"See," Dad says. "Avocados. I never would have guessed that. The key to understanding women is not to try."

Hmm. Maybe my dad is the real Svengali.

"Are you having gal problems?" he asks.

"Dad, no one calls them *gals*."

"Yeah, Dad," my mom says.

"Whatever you call them," Dad says, "Shane, just remember this: We all put our pants on one leg at a time."

"I know. Thanks, Dad. I'm not sure that applies here, though."

It may have taken them a while to figure it out, and they may claim to have no idea what the other is thinking, and the road may be rocky at times, but my parents have achieved the type of relationship that I can only dream of.

It's inspirational, but also depressing to think that I will never experience it myself.

41

I'VE BEEN FEELING unsettled about how I left things with Adam. Our little talk outside anime club unleashed a torrent of consequences that he and I never really discussed. I'm a bit uneasy about how it all went down. And since Jak has not returned my affections, I asked Adam if he could meet up so I could figure out how we got to this point in the first place.

The courtyard in front of school is mostly deserted. In order to chat with Adam I had to wait until after ECX (Extracurricular Extreme, which is now officially a thing). All the normal students have long since gone home or are gathering at the baseball field behind the school for today's consequential playoff game against Valley Hills.

When Adam arrives, I notice that he has contacts in and

is no longer wearing the Clark Kent glasses I picked out for him. Perhaps Rebecca, like Jak, thought he looked better au naturel.

"Hey, man," I say.

"Hey, Shane," he says as he joins me at one of the cement tables.

"How's Rebecca?" I ask.

"She's good. Really good. She'll actually be out here in a minute."

"Oh. Okay."

Numbers one and two in the race for valedictorian, Adam and Rebecca took to each other almost immediately and are now inseparable.

"I guess I better get right to it then," I say. "When I told you that I thought I was having feelings for Jak . . ."

"Yeah?" he says.

"I never said you should stop seeing her."

"You didn't have to. I knew what you meant."

"But how could you have known what I meant if *I* didn't even know what I meant?"

"Wait," Adam says, "so you're not in love with her?"

I pause.

"How do you know I'm in love with Jak?"

"Well, at first I didn't. Because I knew you guys were just friends and had never hooked up. Otherwise I never would have tried to flirt with her in the first place. But after we talked at anime club, I knew. That's why I backed off."

"But *I* didn't even know I was in love with her then!"

"It didn't really matter. If you were interested, I couldn't get in your way. You've done so much for me. I could never do that to you."

"What about Jak?" I ask.

"Listen, Jak is great. We had an awesome time together. But it was really, really short. Like a couple of dates. And then Rebecca came along. I felt bad about Jak, but to be honest, she didn't really seem all that upset when we stopped hanging out, so I thought everything was cool between us. Why? Is she mad?"

"No, not at you. More like confused. But I think that's water under the bridge."

"And what about you two?" he says. "You're in love with her. That's awesome!"

"Well, we're kinda in a holding pattern."

"Not so awesome."

"There's one more thing, Adam."

"Yeah?"

"I knew that Rebecca and Harrison used to date and I didn't tell you. I should have said something. I feel like I left you hanging out to dry."

"Hey, listen, if you had said something, I probably never would have even *talked* to Rebecca. Harrison terrifies me."

"But you and Rebecca are good?"

"We're great. I can't believe everyone got all upset about the Galgorithm. It really works! And Rebecca couldn't care less about the whole scandal thing. Basically, I owe you everything, Shane."

I spot Rebecca exiting the school and heading toward us.

"I was happy to help," I say. "But she's coming."

Adam turns around and waves to his girlfriend. I'm glad we cleared the air. When Rebecca reaches the table, pretty in pink seersucker shorts and a white polo shirt, I can't help but beam with pride at how well that doofus has made out.

"Hey, babe," she says to Adam. He gives her a kiss without standing up because he's almost already at her eye level anyway. She says hi to me and then sits down.

"What are you two doing?"

"Oh, you know, just guy talk," I say.

"Did you know that Shane is in love with Jak?" Adam says. Rebecca gasps. "You are?"

"Adam, what the hell, man?"

"Was that supposed to be a secret?"

"I mean, I guess not." I'm surprised Rebecca doesn't already know. Seems like the rest of the planet does.

"So what's going on with you guys?" Rebecca asks.

"Nothing right now."

"I could totally see you together," she adds.

"Yeah," I say. "I know."

I observe Rebecca and Adam nuzzle and smile at each

other for a few moments. Another reminder of what I *don't* have. I'm about to leave and give them a little privacy when I look up, and my stomach sinks.

"Crap."

"What?" Adam says.

I motion to the side of the courtyard. Harrison is stomping toward our table. He's only wearing the top half of his baseball uniform, boxers, and untied cleats. The latter *click-clack* against the courtyard floor.

We all stand up as he approaches, a weird move by us that's equal parts fear and deference.

"I'm about to play the biggest game of my life," Harrison says, "and I have to hear about you guys hanging out out here?"

It's unclear if the "you guys" he's referring to is Adam and Rebecca or me and Rebecca or just anyone with a pulse.

I, for one, am sick of this nonsense.

"How did you even know where we were?" I say pointedly. "We've been here for like five minutes."

"You know what, Chambliss," Harrison says, "I never got to congratulate you on that little write-up in the *Chronicle*. Good job, Romeo."

"I think you mean Cupid."

"Shut up," Harrison snarls. Then he turns to Rebecca: "Rebecca, why are you doing this to me?"

I find myself actually feeling bad for Harrison. Sure, he's got a funny way of showing it, but obviously he has strong feelings for Rebecca. Why else would he be out here half-naked? Meatheads get lovesick too.

"Harrison," Rebecca says, "we've been over this a million times."

Adam steps in front of Rebecca, like a boss. "Leave her alone," he says. I'm pretty impressed.

Harrison is undeterred. "Rebecca, you *know* why we had to be a secret. You can't blame me for that."

"Well, *we* don't know why," I say. "Why don't you tell us what the hell is going on?"

Harrison starts to crack his knuckles. Rebecca turns to me. "My dad works for Pacifica Oil."

"Um," I say. "Okay. I don't know what that is."

"It's a giant, horrible oil company that pollutes the air," Harrison says. "My moms have been protesting them for years."

I remember spying on Harrison and Rebecca at the house party. *This* is what they were arguing about.

"It's an *energy* company, Harrison," Rebecca says. "And I'm sorry your moms don't like it, but I bet they like computers and air-conditioning and gas for their cars."

"I couldn't have them find out about us," he says. "They would have killed me. It's like dating the enemy's daughter. And you know we drive electric cars."

Adam isn't quite sure what to make of all this, so he stays silent.

"Harrison, don't you think you're taking this a little too far?" I say.

"What? You think I'm some dumb jock? You think just 'cause I play baseball I don't care about Mother Earth? What do you think the field is made of?"

"Um . . . earth?" I stammer.

"Grass, you idiot!"

I recoil. I really have no idea what to do at this point.

"Everything was fine until I started seeing you around," Harrison says to me.

"Harrison, I had nothing to do with any of this. Are you still carrying a grudge from seventh grade? Because I didn't even see the girl you were talking about. Ask the rabbi! I'm sure he remembers. It's probably the only time he's ever had to eject someone from the synagogue."

Harrison evaluates the situation in front of him. There's no logical way out. If anything he should be mad at Adam, but instead he's just mad at the world.

"You all think you're better than me, don't you?" he steams. "You all think you're better than me! But you're not! Especially not you!"

He shoves his finger in Rebecca's face.

Adam pushes Harrison's arm away.

Harrison shoves Adam.

Rebecca pleads, "Leave him alone!"

Adam's adrenaline surges, and I can't believe it . . . but he throws a punch!

Unfortunately, it's a wild haymaker that Harrison easily sidesteps.

Now Adam is off-balance, and Harrison effortlessly pushes him to the ground.

Then Harrison turns his attention to me.

"This is *your* fault, Shane! You did this! You think you're better than me!"

He's screaming at me in his underwear and the whole thing is just insane. I try to reason with him with the only advice I can think of that seems tailor-made for this situation.

"Listen, Harrison. Relax. I don't think I'm better than you. We all put our pants on one leg at a time."

And that's when he winds up and punches me in the face.

42

GETTING CLOBBERED IN THE face is not as dramatic as it looks in the movies. I didn't heroically absorb the blow like Liam Neeson. No, I immediately crumpled to the ground in a heap. I bled. I whimpered. Harrison fled the scene immediately. I later found out that he hurt his hand on my skull, couldn't pitch, and we lost the playoff game. So, good times had by all.

Adam and Rebecca helped me get home, but I got the feeling they couldn't wait to be alone together. Adam stood up for Rebecca and threw the first punch. Even though he missed by a long shot and got shoved to the pavement instead, he scored major points. I expect him and Rebecca to have a long and happy relationship.

I'm not so fortunate. I'm lying on the floor of my bedroom

with an ice pack on my eye. I'm trying to keep the swelling down as much as possible. If I'm lucky, it won't look so bad by the time my parents come home from work. The last thing I need is for them to make a big deal out of it or call the school. I'll just tell them I fell. I was never the most coordinated kid anyway.

There's a crack in my ceiling that I've never noticed before, probably because I don't usually lie on the floor. It starts off pretty small and then forks into a bunch of secondary cracks. It gets worse the farther you go. Kind of like my high school career and my life in general.

My phone rings, and I see that it's a FaceTime request from Jak. I hold the ice pack on my eye with one hand, hold up my phone with the other, and accept the request. She gasps when she sees me on-screen.

"Oh my God! I just heard. Are you okay?"

"Yeah," I say. "It looks worse than it is."

"Take the ice pack off so I can see your eye."

I do.

She gasps again.

"Is it bad?" I ask. It's hard to tell on the tiny image of myself in the corner of the screen.

"Well," Jak says, "that depends on your definition of bad."

"Wonderful."

"The good news is that you can't get any uglier."

"That's a relief."

I put the ice pack back on.

An outside observer might not sense anything amiss in this conversation. But I can tell that things are not the same. In the week since our encounter in the street, Jak and I have pretended to go about things like normal. But Jak is faced with the twin burdens of still being annoyed with me about the Galgorithm *and* knowing that I'm in love with her. Yes, we're joking around on the phone. But it's not as fluid and familiar as it once was.

"Do you need anything?" Jak asks. "Do you want me to come over?"

"No. It's okay."

My head is starting to throb.

"Shane?"

"Yeah?"

"You can't be mad at me," she says.

"I'm not mad at you. What makes you think I'm mad at you?"

"I know you, Shane."

"You know how I feel."

"You promised me it wouldn't be weird."

I did promise that. But it's just been getting weirder and weirder each day.

"I know," I say. "I'm trying. It's hard."

"I don't want to fight with you anymore," Jak says. "But don't think this has been easy for me, either. I'm the responsible one in our friendship. It's the worst."

"Really? *You're* the responsible one, Jak?"

"Shane, you do realize that you're not supposed to put the ice pack directly on your face, right? You're supposed to put a towel under it. You're turning red."

"*You* put a towel under it."

"That doesn't make any sense."

There's a lull in the conversation. There never used to be *any* lulls in our conversations. We could talk for hours without anyone ever taking a breath. But now we're just staring at each other via FaceTime and neither of us knows what to say.

I feel like senioritis is pervading all aspects of my life. I can barely bring myself to go to class anymore. And me and Jak . . . now that I know that we can't be together, it seems like we're just going through the motions.

Jak sighs. "It's tough for me to see you like this," she says.

"You can fix that, Jak. You can change it. You can tell me you feel the same way about me. Then I won't look so depressed."

"I meant it's tough for me to see you with a swollen eye."

"Oh."

Another lull. We're trying too hard. We're not on the same page. Our best friend telepathy is gone. It makes me incredibly sad.

"I wish we could go back in time," I say. "Before I said anything, before I was outed, before the Galgorithm, before Voldemort. Before everything changed."

"So, like eighth grade?"

"Exactly. Eighth grade. I think that's when life peaked. Girls weren't an issue. Me and you were buddies."

"It was simple."

"Yeah."

"Of course," Jak adds, "in eighth grade you were covered in acne. Like, head to toe. I didn't even want to be seen with you."

"I'll take acne over this any day."

I remove the ice pack from my face again.

"How does it look now?"

"You've still got a couple of pimples. One on your nose—"

"Not my acne! My eye!"

"Go easy, Chambliss. I'm just messin' with you."

"I know."

I'm glad Jak still cares enough to tease me.

"You want to know how it looks?" she says. "It looks like you got punched in the face by the starting pitcher of the baseball team. Or former starting pitcher, now that we lost."

Another lull.

Jak looks at me, and all I want to know is what she's thinking. Deep down I hope and pray that she's not telling me everything. She's ten blocks away, yet her image is being bounced to space and back. There's meaning in her face that's lost in the journey, that I can't parse right now and may never be able to.

My friendship with Jak has survived tough times. But not

anything like this. We're out of sync and out of sorts. I want her to forgive me. I want her to love me back. I want her to be lying next to me.

Alas, as the girl with the bar code tattoo once told me: Life is easier said than done.

43

I'M SITTING IN THE CAFETERIA by myself with a black eye and a broken heart.

All the upperclassmen who have off this period have left campus to get lunch, and most of the underclassmen, who technically aren't allowed to leave school grounds, have joined them. It's the first of June, and with summer so perilously close all rules are going out the window.

I haven't brought food with me, nor have I bought anything. I'm not hungry. I'm just staring out at the sun-drenched lawn that borders the cafeteria. Even the squirrels scatter at the sight of me, probably noticing my eye and thinking I'm a giant raccoon.

I've been beaten up inside and out. Besides the occasional nerd who solicits me for dating advice (which I don't give) and the handful of allies who have remained loyal, I am essentially a pariah in Kingsview. I've resolved to serve out the rest of my time in high school as a weird loner.

My parents warily accepted my explanation that my injury was the result of an errant doorknob. Harrison told his coaches he injured his hand during a bench-clearing brawl (that he himself sparked) earlier in the playoffs. I guess that was better than admitting he got into a fight off the field. I told Adam and Rebecca not to snitch on him. Things are bad enough. I don't need to get blamed for the misfortunes of our baseball team too.

This may be the lowest point of my entire life. I'm just plain wallowing in it.

But even the darkest days can be brightened. Even the gloomiest forecast can be wrong.

And today that hope, that ray of sunlight, comes in the form of two bubbly sophomores who enter the cafeteria holding hands and looking for me.

Hedgehog and Balloon.

I can't believe my eye (the other is swollen shut) when they sit down across from me. I haven't seen either of them in weeks.

"Please tell me this isn't some sort of sick joke," I say.

Anthony shakes his head. "Nope. Hedgehog and Balloon are back!"

I still think they're playing a trick on me until Brooke starts to nod.

"It's true," she says.

I literally pump my fists overhead and cheer. "Yes! You don't understand how happy this makes me."

Brooke smiles and rubs the back of Anthony's neck, below his spiky hair.

"So . . . ," I say, "are you gonna make me beg? Tell me what happened!"

"Well, ever since the article came out, I've been thinking," Brooke says. "What's the most important part of a relationship? Is it *how* you got there? Or is it that you got there at all?" She looks lovingly at Anthony. "And I realized that it doesn't matter how Hedghog and I got together. All that matters is that we *are* together and we belong together."

"That's what I've been trying to tell you!"

"I know, Shane. But I had to figure it out for myself. I got a little caught up in the scandal of it all. And I still think the whole Galgorithm thing is a bit creepy. But you're right, the fact that Anthony cared enough about me to *be* creepy in the first place is pretty darn romantic."

She kisses him on the cheek.

"And you told her . . . ?" I ask Anthony.

"Everything," he says. "I told her everything. That you helped me figure out what her interests were. That you helped me write all those text messages. Everything."

"They were your words," Brooke says to me, "but they were coming from Hedghog's heart. So I guess what I want to say to you, Shane, is *thank you*. Thank you for being Anthony's guide and advisor and messenger. Thank you for bringing us together."

"Yeah, man," Anthony adds, "thank you. Me and Balloon have had our ups and downs. But we would be nothing without you."

"It was my pleasure, guys. Really. I'm glad it all worked out."

I can't tell if I'm tearing up or if my shoddy eyelid is just leaking. Probably a little of both.

"Is your eye okay?" Anthony asks. "We heard the rumors about Harrison. What a tool."

"Yeah, yeah, it's nothing," I say. "Sometimes a good punch clears your head." (This has not been the case with me, of course. Things are hazier than ever.)

"I also wanted to let you know that I took the article off the newspaper website," Brooke says. "I know that's probably too little too late, but I thought it was the right thing to do since I kinda didn't ask you for your side before publishing it. Also, possibly committing libel in high school probably won't help my investigative reporting career."

I chuckle. "I appreciate that, Brooke."

"The comments section was quite . . . colorful, to say the least," she adds. "But with it all gone at least you'll be that much harder to google."

"Thank you."

"Um, and . . . ," Anthony starts.

"Don't," I say. "You don't need to apologize for being one of Brooke's sources for the article. If I were in your shoes, I would have also spilled my guts. 'Deny till you die' is just a stupid saying."

"Oh, thank God," Anthony says. "I have been racked with guilt for weeks. My hair has been falling out."

I can only imagine what *that* nightmare scenario looks like.

"It's all good, buddy. I like to think you two did me a huge favor. Me? A dating guru? What a joke. I don't know anything. And I can't even get my own life in order."

"Shane," Brooke says, "that's crazy. Think about how many people you've helped."

"Yeah," Anthony says, "you can't retire. Guys like me need you!"

"Hmmm," I say. "Well, maybe I could get an eye patch and be the dating pirate. 'Excuse me, *arrr!* you a Gemini?'"

Brooke breaks out laughing at my imitation. And, wouldn't you know it, she sounds exactly like a squeaky balloon.

"So what's next for you, Shane?" Anthony asks.

"Well, first I'm gonna take some Advil because right now I see two Hedgehogs and three Balloons. After that, well, we'll see. You guys have given me a little bit of hope."

Sometimes, that's all you need.

44

I BURST INTO THE TEACHERS' lounge and start scanning the room. I'm on a mission. But I'm also disheveled and have a black eye, so all the teachers in the lounge are wondering why a feral student is going rogue in their private area.

Buoyed by Hedgehog and Balloon's reconciliation, I've come here to see if I've still got it. Maybe I can still make a difference.

At first I think I've come up empty. I stalk through the lounge without finding what I'm looking for. Finally I reach the kitchenette in the back. Inside are a coffee machine, a fridge, a two-person table, and Deb sitting with her back to me, reading her iPad. Her seemingly floor-length hair is unmistakable. Bingo.

"Ms. Solomon," I say, "can I talk to you for a second?"

Deb turns around to look at me. "Oh my. What happened to your eye?"

"It's nothing."

"Is that from the same boy who was harassing you in the Student Council office?"

"No," I lie. "This was just an accident. Thank you, by the way, for helping me that time. Everything is fine, though."

"Okay," she says, remaining unconvinced. "What can I do for you?"

I enter the kitchenette area and sit across the table from her.

"It's Mr. Kimbrough," I say.

"Shane." She lowers her voice. "I don't think we should talk about this right now." As in, *all my coworkers are in the other room.*

"It won't take long," I say, trying to be as discreet as possible.

"You shouldn't be involved, Shane. You shouldn't even be in here."

"Please let me say what I have to say. You need to hear it."

"All right," she says, crossing her arms.

"First you should know that this is coming from me. He doesn't even know I'm here. It's just that Mr. Kimbrough, um, Bob . . . he's great. He's a good teacher and a great guy. I know he gets a little carried away sometimes and is a little over the top, but that's just because he cares about you so much. I've never met anyone with such a heart of gold."

"I appreciate you saying all this, Shane. Bob is lucky to

know you. He really is. It's just . . . that *formula*. That algorithm. It was too much. And too public."

"I know," I say. "The texting. And the 'moves.' It's a little creepy. But that's *my* fault. All those things were stupid stuff *I* told him. He only posted it because he was excited. He was so happy when he was around you. I just think it was his misguided attempt to share some of that happiness with the world. His heart was in the right place. And it's a big heart."

She looks at me like she's possibly considering my plea.

"You have to give him another chance, Ms. Solomon. I promise you he's worth it."

Suddenly another voice is heard.

"Shane? What are you doing here?"

We look up to see Mr. Kimbrough.

"Your eye! What happened?"

"Nothing. I'm fine."

He enters the kitchenette area as well.

"Hey, Deb," he says.

"Hi, Bob. Shane here was just telling me some very nice things about you."

Mr. Kimbrough looks at me, ashen. Then to Deb: "I swear I didn't put him up to it. I—"

"It's okay," Deb interjects. "I know. It's all right."

"Mr. Kimbrough," I say, "I was just telling her that the whole Galgorithm thing was my fault and that she shouldn't blame you for it and that you got a little carried away and that she should give you another chance."

"Well, I think a *little* carried away might be a bit of an understatement," he says.

Everyone chuckles, and this thankfully cuts the tension just a bit.

"I'm grateful for you coming here, Shane, and for everything you've done, but I can handle this myself." He turns to Ms. Solomon. "Deb, I know I've said this before, but I'm sorry again for my behavior. It was inappropriate. It was immature. It was downright one three five seven nine."

Deb and I both look at him quizzically.

"Odd. My behavior was downright odd."

I shake my head, but Deb laughs. I guess in a weird, teachery way, Mr. K. can be quite charming.

"I would love to go out with you again," he continues, "under more . . . normal circumstances. But if you would prefer to just be friends and coworkers, I totally understand."

Taking the high road as always. Good for you, Bob. Now Deb will take the bait, accept your apology, and be so impressed that she agrees to take you back. Happy ending for all!

Deb smiles. "Bob, I've really enjoyed our time together. You're sweet and funny, and I love your math jokes."

Mr. K. looks at me as if to say: *See, at least someone appreciates them!*

"But," she continues, "I think I would like to just be friends.

It would be so much less complicated. It doesn't mean I don't care about you."

Mr. K. nods his head solemnly. "I understand," he says.

They share a tender little moment.

But I'm having none of it.

"What do you mean, you understand?" I exclaim. "This isn't how it's supposed to go!"

Bob and Deb look at me like the naive teenager I am. "Things don't always work out the way you want them to," Mr. K. says. "But it's not always a bad thing. It's just the way things are."

Deb adds: "Bob's right. You're something else, Shane. I've never met a student quite like you."

Mr. K. nods in agreement.

I stamp my feet like a child.

"Are you gonna be okay?" Deb asks me.

I honestly don't know the answer to that question. So I say the first thing that comes to mind. "Does this mean you're gonna start giving pop quizzes in history again?"

Deb furrows her brow at first, having no idea what I'm talking about. "Ah," she says, "right. Your friend Jak is in my class. Well, tell Jak she has nothing to worry about. And I didn't even count her as absent that day she cut." She smiles. "Now you should probably get to your next period."

Deb stands up, next to Bob.

I stand as well.

"Thank you for everything, Shane," Bob says.

I give them one last look before I leave. I used to avoid Mr. Kimbrough when he needed advice. Now I want nothing more than to see him and Ms. Solomon together. He seems content to just be friends with Deb, but I hate the fact that he's accepted defeat.

I guess he's right: Not everyone gets what they want.

And I'm resigned to the same fate.

45

I TRUDGE BACK TO MY LOCKER. The next period has started, and the senior hallway is empty. I open my locker and just stare into it blankly. The day has already been a whirlwind. *Only a few more weeks of this,* I try to reassure myself.

I can't sit in a classroom right now. I also don't want to be alone. I want to text Jak and see if she'll cut and meet me to hang out. Then I reconsider. Seeing her but not being with her is just too painful. My head is spinning. I should really go to class. My truancy has become chronic, even for a senior.

I close my locker and then literally jump and grab my heart. Tristen is just standing there, out of nowhere, like in a horror movie.

"What the!" I yelp.

"Hey," she says.

"Tristen, you scared the crap out of me."

"You've been avoiding me."

"It's not avoiding if I told you directly that I can't see you anymore."

"You didn't mean that."

Oh boy. I have been doing my best to end things with Tristen amicably. I've really been giving it the ol' college try. But she refuses to let me go. Yes, I may have slipped up a little bit in the parking lot. But I quickly came to my senses and told her we were through. Since then I've been making sure I'm not giving her the wrong impression. She just keeps coming back, like a hot zombie.

"What are you doing here?" I ask.

"I just wanted to see how your eye was."

"Well, now you can see: It's swollen and gross."

"I actually think it's really sexy."

Of course you do.

Sometimes I hate myself. After all, 99.99 percent of me knows that Tristen isn't right for me. But even after everything that's happened, there's *still* that .01 percent saying, *Hey, listen, Jak is out of the picture; why not?* I hate that .01 percent of me. I hate the testosterone that courses through my body, over which I seem to have no control.

"You wanna sneak into an empty classroom?" she asks.

I pause, but quickly gather myself. "No, Tristen. I don't

want to sneak into an empty classroom. Please. I'm begging you. Leave me alone."

Tristen does not leave me alone. Instead she moves in closer and starts caressing my bruised face.

And just when I think that this already terrible moment, in this absolutely dreadful month, of this totally disastrous year, in my increasingly meaningless life, could not get any worse, I see *him*: my sworn enemy, Harrison, fully clothed this time, walking toward us down the hall.

I briefly consider using her as a human shield, but I pry Tristen off me instead.

"We just have a way of bumping into each other, don't we, Chambliss?" Harrison says when he gets to my locker. "I'm glad I was running late for class."

He doesn't look very glad. I don't say anything.

"Hey, Tristen," Harrison says.

"Hello," she replies.

She puts her hand on my arm.

I make a calculated gamble and say, "Tristen, Harrison is the one who did this to my eye."

Who knows? Maybe she'll kill him. That could work.

She caresses my face again. "You did this?" she asks Harrison. "Why?"

"He doesn't know how to mind his own business," he says.

"That's a lie," I say to Harrison. "I've done nothing *but*

mind my own business. Rebecca is gone. Let her go. I'm not the problem."

"Oh yeah?" Harrison says. "How about the fact that I sprained my hand and couldn't pitch? I almost lost my scholarship."

"Really? You're gonna blame *me* for punching me in the face and hurting your hand?"

"Yeah, that's just crazy," Tristen adds, being an expert herself.

Harrison grits his teeth and begins to crack the knuckles on his good hand.

Witnessing me about to get pummeled turns Tristen on, because what doesn't? She holds me closer.

And that's when, by the grace of God, I have two epiphanies:

One, Tristen and Harrison are both bullies.

And two, *they belong together.*

How could I have been so dense? Here we have two of the most attractive people in school. They keep running into each other. They're both obsessed with me. They both have a few screws loose. They both want to save the world. Tristen, for all her psychosis, is still a good person deep down—and she must be lonely. Harrison, despite his bloodlust, is really just nursing a broken heart (in addition to a sprained hand). It was meant to be!

I peel Tristen off me once more and try my best to keep Harrison at bay.

"Guys," I say, "I want you to hear me out. I think, maybe, what you're both looking for is right in front of you."

"What are you talking about?" Harrison bristles.

"Tristen here may seem like just a pretty face—" I say.

"Thank you," she interrupts, mistaking this for a compliment.

I continue: "But this summer she's doing both Habitat for Humanity *and* helping dolphins in the Congo."

"Technically Gabon," she says.

"Technically Gabon," I clarify.

"And Tristen, you may only know Harrison as the star of our baseball team, or former star."

Harrison growls.

I press on: "But he is actually quite committed to conserving natural resources. Right?"

There's a moment of silence . . . but then Harrison engages.

"Did you know those dolphin-safe labels on cans of tuna aren't regulated?" he says to Tristen. "They basically don't mean anything."

She perks up. "No, I didn't know that! I love tuna fish. Does that mean all those cans of tuna are hurting dolphins?"

"You're probably fine," he says. "But after you finish with the cans, I hope you—"

"Recycle them," they say simultaneously.

A spark flies.

"I hate dolphins *and* recycling," I interject for emphasis. It's ignored.

"Of course," Tristen says to Harrison, "I always recycle. I have like six bags of soda bottles in my trunk I'm gonna recycle after school."

"Really?" Harrison says, as he steps toward Tristen and I slowly back away. "Do you want company? I can carry everything."

Tristen glances at Harrison's biceps. Then they lock eyes.

"But what about Shane?" Tristen asks, suddenly turning and remembering little old me.

"Who, me?" I reply from halfway down the hall. "Don't worry about me. You have my blessing. Please."

Tristen, incredibly, is satisfied by this, and turns back to Harrison. He, on the other hand, is now glowering at me.

"Are we even?" I ask.

Harrison loses focus and sneaks a peek at Tristen's cleavage. Total kryptonite.

"Even," he mumbles, and I can sense he's already forgotten his own name.

I backpedal the rest of the way down the hall.

They are lost in each other's eyes and are finally out of my hands.

Sweet relief.

46

IT'S A BREEZY BUT WARM Saturday night. The kind of night that should be filled with parties and hijinks. I always figured my senior year would wind down in a haze of booze, girls, and fun. Instead, none of those things are present and I'm driving around aimlessly with Reed.

My eye has finally healed enough for me to show my face in public outside school. But things with Jak are still frayed, and everyone else seems to be busy with their significant others or scrambling for prom dates or cramming for finals. I've given up on it all. Reed told me he had news, so I figured I would pick him up and we'd make a night out of it. Some night. Reed has mostly been silent as he sits in the passenger seat of my Jeep.

"We've been driving in circles for half an hour," I say. "Either tell me the news or let's pick a destination."

Reed takes a deep breath. "I've been talking to Marisol," he says.

"Oh," I say.

Reed has been pretty mum about Marisol ever since I tried to inspire him to win her back. He never brought it up, so I just assumed the worst.

"I decided to end things," he says.

I cock my head. "What do you mean *you* decided to end things?"

"Well, after I explained to her what the Galgorithm was really about, and she had a chance to let it all sink in, she forgave me."

"Nice."

"She said that she was actually flattered that I had gone to such great lengths to win her over. I told her I would have followed a thousand Galgorithms if it meant we could be together."

"So she's not mad."

"Nah. She said everyone at school kinda got worked up about it, and she just got swept up in that. She wanted to give it another try."

"So what do you mean *you* ended it?"

"Well, I decided I'm not ready to be in a relationship. Now that I know what it's like, I mean. Marisol was my first girl-friend. And it was amazing. But I told her she'd be better off with someone else."

"Why on earth would you say that?"

"Because I feel like I've found a higher calling."

I glance over at Reed in the passenger seat. He's adopted a middle ground between his mom-certified wardrobe and the more fashionable attire I picked out for him. He looks good now. Upbeat and comfortable in his own skin. Even his posture looks better.

"A higher calling?" I ask. "You're gonna become a priest?"

"No," Reed says. "Even better. I'm gonna become you."

"Huh?"

"I wanna be your successor."

I do a double take.

"My successor?"

"Yeah. I want to take over where you left off. I want to use everything you taught me. I want to help people find love. I wanna reboot the Galgorithm."

A million thoughts cross my mind, and I struggle to process them while continuing to drive in my lane.

"But Reed, you know as well as anyone that the Galgorithm isn't real. That thing Mr. Kimbrough created was a joke. I never wrote down any of my *actual* methods."

"But I did."

Reed holds up his little notebook.

Of course.

"I've been keeping notes from day one," he says. "Including some stuff you told only me. What I have in here is more exhaustive and more accurate and more secret than anything that's online. This is like Galgorithm 2.0. And the world deserves to see it."

I shake my head and smile in disbelief.

"I was also thinking," he continues, "that this doesn't just have to help guys. You have plenty of tips that will work for girls, too. Especially if it's all about confidence and being present. There's no reason why I can't offer girls a 'secret formula' into *our* minds."

"So . . . ," I say. "Like a *Guy*gorithm."

"Yes! *Guygorithm.* I need to write that down."

He scribbles in his notebook.

"Are you sure you're ready for this, Reed?" I ask. "Being known as a dating expert is a lot of pressure."

"Well, maybe it's not so much about advising and coaching. Maybe it's more of a matchmaking service. You know, finding the right girl and the right guy and bringing them together. Plus relationship advice. You did all of that, too, right?"

"Yeah," I say. "True." I choose not to mention the times this went horribly awry, or, in the case of me and Jak, the time it failed completely.

"How about this," he says. "'Reed Wanamaker: Teen Matchmaker.'"

He lets that hang in the air for a moment.

"I must admit," I say, "that does have a nice ring to it."

"I gotta get business cards."

"Rebecca Larabie has a guy who does that. I'll get you the info."

Reed nods. "Noted."

"Just promise me you won't get in over your head," I say.

"I promise. But listen, I'm only gonna do this if you say it's okay."

"Are you asking for my blessing?"

"Come on, Shane. You're graduating, not dying. I would never want to do anything without your permission. What if you want to get back in the game in college?"

"Oh no. One thing is certain. I'm retired for good. Never again. You have my blessing, Reed. Just don't make the same mistakes I did."

"Tell me."

"Dealing with people's emotions is an art. Not only do your clients need to know that, but *everyone* needs to know that. It's very easy for outsiders to misunderstand what we do. Er, what you're gonna do."

"I'm gonna be completely transparent," he says. "I'm even gonna charge. I'm offering a real service; why shouldn't I get paid for it?"

That's a fair point.

"Well, then," I say, "I'm happy to pass the torch to you. Welcome to the love business, Reed."

I pat him on the shoulder.

"Thanks, Shane. I really appreciate it. Also . . . remember when the Galgorithm was exposed and all those people messaged you asking for advice?"

"Yeah . . ."

"You think maybe you could forward them on to me? Those are potential clients."

I laugh to myself.

"Sure thing."

We continue driving as Reed, perhaps the unlikeliest of protégés, jots down notes about his new endeavor. I wish him well.

He finishes writing and closes the notebook.

"So what's the latest with Jak?" he asks.

Lately, Reed has also become the unlikeliest of confidantes. I've pretty much kept him up to speed on all the Jak drama. He's proven to be quite the listener.

"There is no update," I say. "Each day is worse. I just can't get her to take a chance on me."

"Huh," Reed mutters to himself. "I guess doctors do make the worst patients."

"What do you mean?"

"I mean it's funny how you can't take your own advice."

"Oh yeah, this whole thing is just hilarious."

"Shane, will you do me the honor?

"Of what?"

"Of being my first client. No charge, of course."

"Please," I say dismissively. "By all means."

"Okay," Reed says. "I will only tell you what a wise man once told me."

I wait for his sure-to-be sage advice.

And then he looks at me with a knowing grin on his face.

"Be different. Notice her. Tell her."

47

THE HALF-MOON ILLUMINATING the sky is partially obscured by a light mist. This is the price we pay for beautiful weather in Southern California: a monthlong stretch of erratic precipitation known as June Gloom.

It's still warm but starting to drizzle when Jak rushes into my backyard.

"I got here as soon as I could," she says breathlessly. "Are you okay?"

I'm standing next to the hammock. "I'm fine," I say. "I'm sorry about the text. I just needed to see you."

"So it's not an emergency?"

"That depends on your definition of emergency."

"I don't understand," she says.

She's wearing skintight jeans and her Led Zeppelin T-shirt.

When she walks toward me, her Chucks make a *crunch crunch crunch* sound in the grass.

"What the . . ."

She stops and bends down to pick up what she's been stepping on. "Are these . . . peanuts?"

"Yeah," I say. "*Amor y cacahuetes.* Remember? Love and peanuts."

"Love and peanuts," she says, nodding.

"Things just haven't been the same between us lately," I say. "I thought this might be a nice reminder of what we used to share."

"It is nice," she says.

Then Jak notices the massive amount of peanuts I have spread throughout the backyard, starting around the hammock in the center and radiating outward. "That's a lot of peanuts," she says.

"Some of them are cashews. It was the best I could do on short notice."

Reed convinced me to drop him off in the middle of town. He told me that he'd get home himself, and that I should follow my heart. I rushed to a grocery store near my house that I knew was still open and cleaned them out of nuts. Thank God my parents have more of a social life than me and are out for the night.

"You're probably gonna get invaded by squirrels," Jak says.

"Let them invade."

She walks closer to me. *Crunch crunch crunch*. She's ten feet away.

"Jak, I just need to say that nothing matters more to me than our friendship. I will always be your best friend. And if nothing else, all I want to do is lie in this hammock with you and stare up at the stars, like old times."

Jak glances at the sky.

"It's raining," she says.

"It'll pass."

She looks at me.

"Your eye is better."

I shake my head. I refuse to be sidetracked. "When we were standing in the street, next to that tree, and I told you how I felt about you, and I asked you if you felt the same way, you said no."

"Yeah . . ."

"Well, I don't believe you."

"Are you calling me a liar?" she asks semiseriously.

"Yes," I say.

"Shane, why would I make something like that up?"

"Because you have a vivid imagination and a lot of time on your hands."

She smiles.

Our skin is damp with drizzle, but the mist is so fine we barely even notice.

"I don't think you're being honest with yourself, Jak."

"How do you know what I'm doing with myself?"

Her phrasing momentarily flusters me. Typical Jak. But I press on.

"Because I know you, Jak. You didn't want me to leave when I crashed your coffee date with Adam. When you held my hand at the smoothie bar, you didn't want to just hold 'the hand that touched Tristen's boobs.' You wanted to hold *my* hand. You didn't get so goddamn drunk at that party because of Adam or because of Tristen. You did it because of me."

"Shane . . ."

"Tell me, right here, right now, with a straight face, that you *don't* have feelings for me."

She doesn't respond.

"Tell me."

"Shane."

"Just tell me and I'll stop bothering you."

"I can't," she says finally.

"Wait," I stammer. "You can't tell me you don't have feelings for me because you *don't*? Or you can't tell me you don't have feelings for me because you *do*?"

Why is it always so much more poetic in the movies?

Jak blinks.

"The second one," she says.

"The second one? The second one is the good one. That means that maybe you *do* have feelings for me!"

"That one," she confirms.

My heart swells. Knowing her as well as I do, I don't know why I ever expected Jak to actually show emotion. Jak doesn't emote. This is like pulling teeth. And I wouldn't have it any other way.

"So, there's something here," I say.

"Yes," she says, biting her lip.

She walks right up to me. *Crunch crunch crunch.*

"For how long?" I ask. "How long have you felt this way?"

"I don't know," she says.

"Have you *always* felt this way?"

"No. I mean, not like this."

"But when I told you that I loved you . . ."

"I didn't know. I didn't know what I was feeling. I just wanted to protect myself."

"Okay . . ."

"I was starting to like you. Like, *like you* like you. But then I got scared."

"Why?"

"Because of what happened with Voldemort. I've seen what happens when you fall for someone. You get in too deep. And then someone gets hurt and someone else gets a horrible nickname."

"That's not gonna happen with us," I say.

"How do you know?"

"Because Jak is the only nickname you'll ever have. I promise."

She manages a smile.

As quickly as it came, the drizzle stops and the mist clears, leaving the half-moon bright in the sky.

"Ever since the party," she says, "ever since you helped me in the bathtub, I don't know. It's just . . . the way you took care of me that night. The way you *always* take care of me."

"If you had only *said* something . . ."

"But then the whole Galgorithm thing happened. Why do you think I was so upset? You hurt me so badly, and I hadn't even opened up to you yet. I imagined what would have happened if I had."

"You know I never meant to hurt you, Jak. You of all people."

"I know. But at the time I decided I could never say anything and just hoped everything worked itself out."

"It didn't work itself out," I admit. "We're not back to normal. But at least now we both know how we feel."

"I was scared," she says. "But the more I thought about it, the more I realized it was *okay* to be scared. Like, maybe it's a good thing, or whatever. Maybe it meant it was real. And then you go and do something like this." She motions to the hammock and the nuts. "I'm not scared anymore."

A drop of rainwater trickles down from her hair onto her forehead. She wipes it away with her wrist.

"Here," I say. "I have something for you." I dig into my pocket and pull out her Fitbit. "Don't worry. It's waterproof."

She extends her arm and I put it on her wrist. Then I hold her hand.

"Shane Xavier Chambliss," she says. "I'm feeling a lot of feelings right now, and it's weird."

"I know. I went through the same thing."

If only she could just *say* the words I need her to say.

Suddenly she pulls her hand away.

"I can't," she says. "I'm the responsible one, remember? I can't jeopardize our friendship again."

"Jak, I don't want to be responsible. I want to be irresponsible. I don't want to be simple. I want to be complicated. I want to be irresponsible and complicated and unpredictable and reckless. That's love."

She looks at me with those unforgettable eyes and says, "Did you practice that speech?"

She's always had a way with words.

"Jak, I would punch you right now if I didn't want to kiss you so badly."

"But what if it doesn't work out?"

"Then we'll deal with it then. We've been through worse."

"Shane," she says, "I can't lose you again."

"Jak, my parents waited five years to be together. We've already waited eighteen. I can't wait any longer. This was meant to be. Voldemort, the Galgorithm, it was all leading to this moment, right now, with you.

She extends her hand to me once again. "I'm ready to lie in the hammock now."

It's about as sentimental as she gets.

I grab her hand and help her into the hammock. *Crunch crunch crunch.* Then I walk around to the other side and get in as well. *Crunch crunch crunch.*

We lie side by side, staring off into the sky.

It's so peaceful.

"My butt is wet," Jak says.

"Mine too."

She holds my hand.

"Shane?"

"Yeah?"

"What if I told you that I didn't want to be #Shak. What if I said that all I want is for you to be my best friend forever and ever, nothing else, nothing more. Would you be okay with that?"

"Jak, I would do anything for you."

It's the truth.

She rolls onto her side, puts her head on my shoulder and her hand on my chest.

"Your heart is racing," she says.

"I'm sorry. I can't help it."

I can feel her breathing on my neck. She throws her leg over mine and climbs on top of me. The hammock wobbles precariously for a moment and then steadies.

She puts both hands on my chest and looks down at me. Her hair is silhouetted beautifully by the moonlight.

I don't think there has ever been a more perfect moment than this one.

"Don't worry," Jak whispers. "I won't ruin it."

Our best friend telepathy has returned.

The cedar trees lining the yard block out all the sound except for our breathing.

"I hear you," she says.

I hesitate. "Did you say I hear you or I *heart* you?"

She contemplates this. "I *said* I hear you. But I meant to say . . . *I heart you.*"

There are three little words I've been waiting forever for her to utter.

And these are close enough.

"I love you too, Jak."

She smiles and looks at my lips.

You don't need a formula to figure out what happens next.

$$\text{👫} = \left(\sqrt{\heartsuit} \times ♀ \right) + \text{👄} \times ♂$$

ACKNOWLEDGMENTS

Like Lord Voldemort and his Horcruxes, I have left little pieces of my soul in each of my five books. *Me You Us*, in particular, was a true labor of love. But it is also the product of extraordinary teamwork, for which I am eternally grateful.

I would like to thank my mom, dad, and sister, Caryn, for being tireless cheerleaders, trusted advisors, and my all-time number-one fans. No three humans could ever be as tolerant or supportive. Your contributions to my life are boundless and unconditional, and inspire me each day. I could not have asked for better parents or a more devoted sister. I love you with all my heart.

My intrepid editor, Sara Sargent, would probably object to my use of the word "intrepid," cross it out, and write: *something funnier?* In truth, she is a whip-smart dynamo who dedicated herself to this project, absorbed many body blows from yours truly, and dished out equal parts comfort and cudgel. First we were strangers. Then we were colleagues. And now we are the best of frenemies.

My agent, Peter McGuigan, is an indispensable part of my career. I can always count on him to dole out sage advice, drop the hammer at the negotiating table, or threaten to beat up unruly fans at my stand-up shows. I am fortunate to have him in my corner, and to have been on the receiving end of so much guidance and so many rounds of beer.

My attorney, Darren Trattner, is the most veteran member of Team Karo and has been calmly steering the ship for more than a decade. The hardest-working man in show business, he still makes time to offer counsel, share wisdom, and take digs at the Yankees. I am perpetually thankful for his diligence, empathy, and insight.

The entire Simon Pulse team has been like a second family, without which this book would certainly not exist. Special thanks to Liesa Abrams, Mara Anasta, Faye Bi, Nicole Ellul, Jessica Handelman, Kayley Hoffman, Mary Marotta, Sarah McCabe, Christina Pecorale, Lucille Rettino, Jennifer Romanello, Teresa Ronquillo, and Carolyn Swerdloff.

A huge thank-you to those who read the book while it was still in its infancy, and those who will continue to sing its praises long after publication: Greg Pedicin, Jeff Greenberg, Josh McGuire, Jessica Regel, Richie Kern, Karen Sherman, Stacey Sakal, Michelle Bontems, Lindsey Rosin, and Katrina Leno.

To my friends and family in New York and Los Angeles: Thank you for having my back all these years, through thick and thin. It means more than you know.

And lastly, to my fans across the country and around the world, thank you for continuing to help make my dreams come true. I promise I'll keep telling jokes as long as you keep laughing. I heart you all.